Table of Contents

Chapter One

Chapter Two

Chapter Three

Chapter Four

Chapter Five

Chapter Six

Chapter Seven

Chapter Eight

Chapter Nine

Chapter Ten

Chapter Eleven

Chapter Twelve

Chapter Thirteen

Chapter Fourteen

Chapter Fifteen

Chapter Sixteen

Chapter Seventeen

Chapter Eighteen

Chapter Nineteen

Chapter Twenty

Chapter Twenty-One

Chapter Twenty-Two

Chapter Twenty-Three

Chapter Twenty-Four

When the Veil Falls

Falls

The Reset: Book Two

By
Joshua Griffith

Cover art by SelfPubBookCovers.com/
Daniela

ASIN: B08L8HRY7R

ISBN: 9781735078427

Contact Joshua Griffith on Facebook

Follow him on Twitter

Or on BookBub

Chapter One

"Ma'am, please come down from there," the police officer ordered through the megaphone.

Eve stood precariously on the ledge of the pedestrian walkway, legs wobbling from the dizzying heights of the St Johns Bridge. She lazily gazed down into the murky waters of the Willamette below as the tears streaked down her wind-burned cheeks from the gusty November winds.

It can be all over, Eve thought to herself.

Flashing red and blue lights lit up the area like a festive Christmas scene against the green paint that covered the bridge as several more Multnomah County squad cars showed up. Off in the distance, the wailing of sirens of a fire truck echoed through the normally tranquil valley. Eve didn't want to make a scene like this. All she wanted was to park near the river, sneak up here, blending in with the other joggers, and take the plunge in the icy waters. She had no choice in the matter as she drove to the bridge. The *passenger* with her kept tormenting her as he always did since she was fifteen. *He* kept her distracted to the point that she missed the side road that led to the river. Eve somehow ended up parking in the middle of St Johns Bridge, clogging traffic.

He is the reason why Eve had been hospitalized multiple times to the point that all the surrounding Emergency Departments knew her by sight. She could tell that the staff treated her differently from the other "normal" patients. The stigma of mental illness was in full swing with each trip. It never failed that Eve found herself in the isolation rooms because they claimed she tried to hurt herself or the staff.

No matter how much she argued or pleaded, Eve couldn't get them to believe that she was trying to protect them and herself from *him*. Her personal demon and tormentor. No matter what she did or where she went, the demon followed her like an undetachable parasite. Eve attempted to smudge her whole body in sage, along with her parent's house, but all it did was keep the demon at a distance from her. Inevitably, *he* returned with even more torments and cruel ways to torture her.

"Ma'am, why are you doing this?" another voice called out from the bullhorn, "I'm officer Diego, what's your name?"

"Eve. Eve Driskell," she replied as she glanced over her shoulder at her would-be savior. *Quite the hunk,* she thought, but then she sighed knowing there would be no future with him or any others for that matter.

The demon chuckled as it hovered beside her, unseen by everyone but Eve, "*You're correct, No one will ever want to be with a freakshow like you. Do you actually believe that cop would want you? No one in their right mind would and you certainly aren't in your right mind.*"

Officer Diego replied back, "Nice to meet you, Eve. Can you explain why you've chosen this path?"

The girl snapped her head towards her personal tormentor and hissed, "Piss off and leave me alone for once in my life!"

"As far as I know, this is the first time I've met you. Why don't you step away from the ledge so we can have a proper chat?"

The demon chuckled next to Eve's ear, *"Yes, step away into oblivion. This can all be resolved and no more time in the hospitals."*

"Why are you doing this? Why must you torment me?" Eve groaned as she clutched her head, not wanting to hear the entity's voice. Officer Diego whispered to several officers before saying, "I'm not here to torment you, Eve. I want to help you. Whatever you are going through isn't worth losing your life."

"Listen to Officer Stud," the demon cooed as it mocked, *"you have more to live for. I don't want to miss out on this fun with you. Live and I will be with you, forever."*

"Fuck off!" Eve snarled as she threw a punch at nothing, at least that's what it seems to all the first responders on the bridge. The demon laughed as she punched again, but this time, a swift gust of wind got her off balance. The troubled girl nearly slipped off and over the ledge.

Eve frantically flailed and snatched a steel cable as people gasped. Most of her body hung off the bridge, like she was windsurfing in the Gorge. Her toes barely touched the metal structure.

Eve could feel tears rolling down her cheeks, embarrassed to be seen in this position. The demon caressed her spine like a lover, causing her to flinch, as it spoke, "*If I were you, I'd let go. I'd be so mortified that all these nice people saw me dancing around up here that I'd rather face the icy depths below than their judgmental stares. Look at them, Eve, and tell me that they see nothing but a freak show.*"

Eve couldn't resist looking into the crowd. People were looking at her either shaking their heads in disapproval or covering their mouths in horror.

Why not let go and give them the show, Eve bitterly thought.

Even though these people were complete strangers wanting to help, Eve knew that they were also cold and miserable, wanting to go back home to their loved ones.

It was all her fault that they were here on this freezing night.

Better to leap off here and let the Willamette swallow me whole, Eve mused, *they can fish my bloated blue corpse out in the spring.*

The demon got face to face with her, grinning with delight, *"Yes! Let these dark thoughts guide you to the right decision. It's quite selfish of you to hang around and cause so much suffering."*

"Eve!" Officer Diego cried out, "I know you are hurting, but I can see that you truly don't want to die. Please, step towards us. No one wants to see you fall."

"Lies!" The demon snorted, *"You and I both know that's not true."*

Eve ignored both the cop and the demon, but her tormentor goaded by adding with a chuckle, *"Look into the minds of the crowd, like I taught you, and see for yourself."*

Eve didn't want to hear the thoughts of others. It was bad enough when they were bombarding her mind without any way to shut them out. It was one of the reasons that her tormentor came to her. It told her that it could help her control the flow of thoughts, but Eve had to accept the entity as a *teacher*.

Eve was desperate and unconditionally accepted it's aid. She just wanted the voices to stop. Little did she know that the demon had other things to teach. Nonstop torment, day and night, as a form of "character building" as it put it.

"Do it and the choice will be simple to make."

Eve begrudgingly closed her eyes and tuned out her surroundings, quieting the rumbling engines coming from the different vehicles and dimming the harsh flashing lights. Immediately, her mind was bombarded with the many voices of the people nearby.

Some had tones of compassion and sadness while others were rude, snarky, bordering on apathy. *Save her* from some or *jump or get off the bridge* was the general message that got through to Eve. Tears painfully streamed down her cold, wind-burned cheeks. All she needed to do was let go so everyone could get back to their lives.

"See? Nobody cares about you. Let go." The demon grinned as he motioned to the swift water below, *"The river will break your fall..."*

Eve intertwined her arms and legs around the icy steel wire with her back to death's edge, shaking and feeling numb. She noticed shadowy movement just beyond her peripheral vision, inching closer to her, when her demonic tormentor suddenly appeared inches from her face, snarling and growling.

It startled Eve, causing her to slip over the edge of the bridge. She desperately grasped onto the steel wire, her legs dangling and feeling like they weighed twice as much. The clattering of footsteps echoed as she felt a great number of hands grabbing ahold of her body.

The demon cackled as it mocked, *"Officer Stud is copping a feel! Do you think he wants to touch you in other places now that you have literally fallen for him?"*

Eve's anger flared as she got dragged to safety. She flailed her arm, glaring at the demon that position itself in front of two of her rescuers, and spat, "Fuck off and leave me alone, asshole!"

Eve could hear someone behind her mutter, "That's gratitude for you, right there, after saving her life. Ungrateful little shit."

Officer Diego pleaded with Eve as he wrangled her arm, "Please stop fighting us, you might hurt yourself."

Eve thrashed her body until her arms were twisted behind her back. She felt someone on top of her as the metallic, clicking of handcuffs were snapped and secured. Several hands changed spots and then, Eve was lifted up to a kneeling position as a heavy blanket was draped around her.

"Indeed, you are an ungrateful piece of shit. You couldn't kill yourself without causing a scene. So pathetic. So weak!" The demon taunted near her ear.

Eve turned her head and attempted to bite the demonic entity, but ended up with her mouth on one of a first responders' forearm. The lady shrilled as Eve clamped down hard, breaking the skin with her teeth, "Get her off me! This crazy bitch is biting me!"

The demon chuckled, "*That's not me you are chewing on, Eve. Now you've gone off the deep end.*"

She let go of the woman, fresh blood coated her mouth. Eve blankly stared at the woman she just bit as she ran to the nearest ambulance. Officer Diego motioned for the EMT crew to bring the gurney. Eve knew what this meant as her tormentor voiced it, "*Looks like someone is going to the hospital once again. At least you can make a grand entrance with those blood-soaked lips.*"

Officer Diego towered over Eve, the compassionate person was gone and now a stern authority figure loomed over her. His steely gaze froze her in place as he commanded, "Eve we are going to stand you up and place your hands in front of you and put these leg irons around your ankles. If you choose to resist us any further, I *will* use the Taser on you. Do we have an understanding?"

Eve meekly nodded as she hung her head in shame. *How did it come to this?* She felt arms and hands grip her limbs tightly as an officer snapped the leg irons on. Another officer wrapped a chain around her waist that has wrists cuffs attached to it.

Once these were secured to Eve's body, Officer Diego coldly ordered, "We are going to uncuff you and put your hands up front now. As I said before, I will *not* hesitate to use the Taser on you. Do you understand?"

When Eve nodded in compliance, Officer Diego motioned to the person behind her. The pressure from the handcuffs was gone but it didn't matter because her arms were guided to her waist, where the next set of restraints dangled. More tears flowed from her eyes as the restraints snapped painfully snug to her wrists, her long, dirty blonde hair matted against her head.

"I don't blame them," the demon commented, *"You're wild, unpredictable, and have proven that you're a danger to yourself and others. I would have the cuffs cutting off the circulation if it were up to me. You won't be going home anytime soon, not after tonight."*

"Why can't you leave me alone?" Eve muttered to the demonic entity.

"It's for your own safety," Officer Diego replied, thinking that she spoke to him, "We're going to have you lay down on the gurney there and take you to the hospital for evaluation. Move."

Eve shuffled quietly toward the gurney, the chain on the leg irons scrapped along the pavement as the demon chuckled, "*You look like a pitiful excuse for a penguin, Eve!*"

Several EMTs buckled her on the gurney once she got situated. Taking no chances, one of the officers held Eve's head down so she wouldn't have an opportunity to bite someone again. As a heavy blanket got unceremoniously tossed over her shivering body, an angry woman got in Eve's face, shaking her forearm as she hissed, "I hope you have a great lawyer, little girl, because I'm going to be pressing charges on you for this! What do you have to say for yourself?"

"I'm so sorry," Eve whimpered, her lips quivering, "I thought I was biting the demon's nose."

"You're bat shit crazy, girl!" The bite victim screeched as she was escorted away from Eve, "I hope they lock you up and toss the keys in the ocean!"

"You make friends well. I'm sure you'll be fine at your next stay in the mental ward."

Just as the gurney was hoisted into the back of the ambulance, through bleary eyes Eve could barely make out a couple of dark humanoid figures watching her. She knew that neither one was her tormentor and definitely wasn't any of the first responders because they both sat on top of a majestic looking horse that had armor plating.

Eve wondered who these entities were and why they chose to be nothing more than spectators. They're probably enjoying the chaos that transpired tonight. Definitely wasn't human or of this plane because people easily moved through them effortlessly. As the EMTs got in the back and closed the doors, Eve felt the cold hands of her tormentor on her shoulders. It looked down upon her with amusement and pleasure as it spoke, *"I've been eavesdropping on the conversations with your* saviors and I've learned of your destination. Would you like to hear it?"

"Yes," Eve sighed, "where are we going to from here?"

"The emergency room first, then jail, for the time being," a male EMT replied matter of fact, "and then the state hospital to get the treatment that you deserve to get."

"What I deserve is to die and be at peace, why couldn't you just let me do that?"

The demon chuckled as the same EMT answered, "You deserve to live and experience life at its fullest. You're so young, what would be so terrible or painful that would make you want to needlessly throw your life away?"

Eve turned her head away from him, closing her eyes and grimacing as her tormentor grazed its sickly claws on her cheek. The bewildered EMT looked on as three scratches appeared, oozing blood as Eve stoically replied, "You know nothing of the pain and torment that I experience daily."

Chapter Two

Eve sat quietly on her cot, repetitively rocking with her arms wrapped around her knees against her chest. She wondered how long her stay in the county jail would last after being in here for the past two days. Given the assault on one of her rescuers, she wasn't sure exactly how long her stay here would be. Eve was worried that when her day came with the judge that he or she wouldn't go lenient on her. She didn't want to spend years behind bars.

Why couldn't they let me die? How is this part of saving my life?

She surveyed the holding cell; it was quite sparse and devoid of any luxuries. Shelves were inlaid into the wall, like tiny cubbyholes. All the cots were attached to the walls, including hers, and had no linens, just weighted blankets and bare pillows. A toilet in full view of others, privacy was not allowed here, especially those considered suicidal. Her outfit consisted of bright orange, county issued clothing and rubber, open-toe shower sandals. Eve debated on using her clothes as a way to asphyxiate herself, to set herself free from her tormentor. Eve saw one glaring obstacle to her exit strategy: there was a camera observing her at all times and an officer would make their rounds.

Despite being watched, Eve never felt safe and secure. Fighting amongst the inmates was a common daily occurrence. She cried, wishing that she wasn't in this place and in her tiny studio apartment. *Unfortunately, that's the problem with wishes, they don't come true,* she bitterly thought. Hope wasn't in her future. Being incarcerated meant that she would be losing her apartment because keeping a job had been a difficult task and she was already several months behind on rent. An eviction notice had been given to her which pushed her forward in her decision to end her life. Eve didn't want to live out of her car or in a homeless shelter.

She was in that situation for almost a year before getting her apartment and she barely survived. Lack of food and resources kept her from moving in the right direction. Jobs were hard to find and those employers that took a chance on her regretted it within a few months. Eve's unseen demon ensured that she acted out and appeared to be a liability, similar to how she behaved on the bridge, with the exception of biting someone. Eve wanted so badly to be rid of her otherworldly tormentor, but didn't know how to do it.

How do you fight what you can't touch?

The jingling of keys brought Eve out of her inner musing as the door to her cell opened. The officer let another inmate into her cell as he stated, "It's a busy week so you're going to have a bunkmate, maybe more. You two play nice, understand?"

The inmates both nodded as the officer closed and locked the cell door. Eve kept a watchful eye on her new cellmate, wondering if she could trust her or not. The woman towered over her with her meaty arms wrapped around her plump breasts. She had spikey bleach blonde hair and tattoos covering her neck and wearing the fine orange jail attire. The portly female eyed Eve and asked, "So, what are you in for, little girl?"

Eve shrugged her shoulders, "Disturbing the peace, assault and battery. How about you?"

The woman chuckled, "Oh a rowdy one, are ya? You don't look like you can hurt a fly. Did you really do that or are trying to be all hard and tough with me?"

"No, I did it, but I wish that I hadn't." Eve answered with shame as she looked away from the large woman, rubbing her arm, "You never said what you're in here for, lady."

"Assault with a deadly weapon and," the inmate got into Eve's face, "murder in first degree."

"Eve is my name," she stated calmly, trying her best not to shake in front of the lady, "What's your name?"

The portly female reached out and grabbed Eve by her scrub collar, yanking her off the cot Eve struggled to free herself, but the woman had a vise-like grip. She felt her feet lift off the ground as she came face to face with this intimidating monster before her.

"I don't have to tell you a damn thing, you understand, little girl?" As Eve quickly nodded, the inmate continued, "I think a little lesson is in order, to show you who's the boss in here."

"What did I do to you?" Eve pleaded, "Whatever it was, I won't do it again."

"Questions from a sniveling whelp, I can tell you aren't what you want me to think you are. I don't like you and your lesson begins..." As the lights shut off in the cell, the woman coldly grinned, "now."

The portly female roughly slammed Eve against the wall and proceeded to punch her in the gut a half dozen times. Eve tried calling for help, but the female inmate covered her mouth as she snarled, "Be silent or you won't live to see breakfast."

Eve wanted to crumble on the cold damp floor, but she was pinned to the wall by her attacker's forearm and her weight. After delivering several more blows, the woman whispered in Eve's ear, "I know the routine here, little girl. Someone will be coming by shortly to check on us. You *will* lay in bed and cry all you want, but if you try to snitch on me, you're a dead girl. Got it?"

Eve half nodded and groaned. The woman smacked the side of Eve's head as she hissed, "You got it?"

Tears painfully streamed down as Eve curtly nodded the best that she could before she was thrown onto her cot. Eve curled up in a fetal position, clutching her stomach as she spastically whimpered in pain. Eve heard laughter by her ear and knew it wasn't coming from her cell mate.

"My aren't you a hot mess. You make friends quickly, don't you? I still say that you should've jumped off the bridge but we both know that you are too weak-minded and pathetic to accomplish that simple task. As a result, look at where you are now."

"Just leave me alone now. I'm not in the mood for your presence," Eve muttered as she grimaced. The female inmate was about to retort when the bright light from a patrolling officer's flashlight shined into the cell. The man looked at both prisoners and asked, "Is there a problem or are you causing trouble again, Adara?"

"No, I'm being a good girl," Adara answered sweetly as she pointed at Eve, "This one is struggling tonight and I was coming over to comfort her. Isn't that true, Eve, my dear?"

Eve stoically nodded, "Yes, I'm struggling with everything because of the demon...and not my new friend here."

"You see?" Adara added with a sweet smile as she sat down on Eve's cot, lovingly stroking her short black hair, "Eve is mentally struggling tonight and I asked her if she wanted to cuddle with me, to keep her company. She was hesitant at first, but in the end, she beckoned for me to join her."

"I'd rather hear it from her own lips. Eve tell me what's *really* going on here?"

"Ooh, this will be good to see you make a choice. Tell the truth and be ready to watch your back from here on out or lie and let Adara cuddle with you, making you her little woman. Choose wisely, but remember this: whatever choice you

make, know that you deserve the consequences because you deserve to be punished."

Eve scrunched her eyelids tightly as she grimaced, knowing that the demon had a point. If Eve spoke up about the assault, then she forfeited her life. If she lied about Adara's wanting to comfort her, then who knows what other forms of humiliation and pain would follow.

"It's... it's like she said. I'm not handling this place mentally and Adara is... showing me kindness...in her own way."

The officer eyed the two prisoners intently before muttering, "Fine. Adara if you *truly* care about Eve's well-being, just know that she's on suicidal protocols. Don't help her in any way that she can use to hurt herself."

Adara coyly smiled as she batted her eyes innocently, "I would *never* dream of letting this little wild flower come to harm. If she wants, I will lie with her here to keep her *demon* at bay."

The demon giggled by Eve's ear, causing her to flinch, which didn't go unnoticed by the policeman, as it whispered, "*I like her, she's smooth and cunning like a demon. I can't wait to watch you two love birds tonight! I can tell that you won't be getting any sleep tonight.*"

"If Eve isn't kept safe during her short stay here," the officer commanded with a firm, but cold voice, "I will have no problem tossing you into cell block 3, with your old friends Corrie, Teri, Latonya, and Red Jayne. Do we have an understanding, Adara?"

Adara stiffened as she took a quick breath while dragging Eve into her bosom, "There is no need for that. This one I will take care of personally. I will dote on her like a lover does in a time of need. Please, don't let them know that I'm here. Is there anything else you need from me?"

"It's too late for that, Adara," the officer chuckled, "word has already reached their collective ears so mind your manners and watch your back. This is your only warning on this matter."

"Got it, boss man!" Adara saluted as he walked away from the cell door. As the sound of the officer's footsteps got fainter to hear,

Adara yanked Eve's head back by her hair. She caressed Eve's face as she spoke, "It seems you're popular for some reason, crazy girl. I know you heard him order me to leave you alone, but you're still mine and will do as I say. I won't kill you and I won't allow you to off yourself because I know that he *will* follow through with the transfer. So, here's what's going to happen: you will do as I say and let me do whatever I want with you because you *are* mine to play with."

"Why must you do this to me?" Eve barely whispered, causing her to wonder if her new *friend* heard her, "Can't we be friends or something? I kept my mouth shut, like you asked. What more do you want from me?"

"We *are* friends. And friends watch out for each other, but you still need to learn your place at my side. If I'm being forced to keep you safe, you'll have to pay for the protection, which requires you to do what I ask of you."

"I don't have any money or cigarettes to give you as payment-"

Adara cut Eve off with a belly laugh, "Oh Eve, you are so sweet and naive. I guess I should spell it out better for you. You're my little bitch in here. Since you can't be my punching bag, I'm going to take payment from your body however I see fit."

The demon hoovered in the air, grinning ear to ear like the Cheshire cat, "*There's a pecking order in this place, Eve, and you're at the bottom. You can always fight this woman, but we both know that you're both weak and pathetic. You will be this one's servant and bed buddy. I know this because I can see her sweet, dark thoughts she has for you. Be a good girl and do what you're told and you may yet leave here alive.*"

"What..." Eve struggled with the words, fearing that she knew the answer, "what do you...wish me to do... for you, Adara?"

Adara's gaze held Eve's as she leaned in and firmly kissed her on the lips. Eve audibly gulped as tears trickled down her sweaty cheeks. Adara murmured as she pressed her lips near Eve's ear, "You best reciprocate the same affection I give you or I *will* get rougher if you keep resisting me."

"I'm sorry, I will try...Adara."

"Good girl," Adara replied as she stood up, pulling Eve off the cot and to her feet, "I say anything to you, you're to refer to me with the endearment 'my love'. Understand, my crazy girl?"

"Yes, Adar-" Eve froze as Adara glared as she amended, "I mean, my love. I'm sorry I'm not use to this sort of thing...my love."

"That's why you need to be taught. You *are* my crazy girl and the lessons I must teach you is part of the price you *must* pay. Now, strip down and get into bed. Don't hesitate or I *will* remove them for you."

Eve gasped in pain as she tenderly pulled her orange scrub shirt off. She let it drop to the floor as she slid her fingers into the hem of the scrub pants. Eve wiggled out of them, letting the pants pool at her ankles. Eve felt self-conscious about being naked in front of anyone. She made it a point to hide from prying eyes in the women's locker room when she was at school.

Eve never had any boyfriends for long enough to see her exposed, nothing but heavy petting and make out sessions, but never got to the point of nudity. Thanks to her demonic tormentor. It always found new ways to cause Eve to scare the guys away with outbursts and "crazy talk" as someone put it.

Eve looked over her shoulder, eyeing the video camera and then back at her *love*. Eve meekly moved towards the cot before Adara barked, "Don't be a slob, crazy girl! Pick up your clothes and put them away neatly. You don't want to give our guards any reasons to be concerned, do you?"

"No, my love," Eve quickly bent down to gather her jail attire, "I'm sorry that I'm a disappointment to you, my love."

"You're a disappointment to everyone, no matter where you go or who you're with, crazy girl! That endearment suits you well. Don't keep your new master waiting." The demon mocked.

As Eve placed her clothes on a small shelf, Adara stood next to her, fully undressed with her clothes in her arms. Eve reached out and took them from Adara, who smiled approvingly as she caressed Eve's bare skin.

"You learn quickly, crazy girl. Already you knew what I wanted you to do before I spoke so this pleases me. Now, get into bed and face me, not the wall, crazy girl."

Eve complied as she laid down on the cot, her back an inch from the wall so Adara would have plenty of room. The little psychic's portly master laid down next to her, Adara eyes wandering, examining her property. The woman's meaty hands groped their way around Eve's delicate features, making her squirm uncomfortably. As a whimper escaped Eve's soft lips, Adara forcefully grabbed her by the jaw as she sneered, "Eve, you're being unresponsive in the way that you're supposed to be with me. This disrespectful attitude you have right now can't go unpunished."

Eve's eyes widened with panic, "No, please, Adara! I'm sorry, please let me make it up to you. I'm just not used to this... this kind of touching."

"You leave me no choice in the matter. I was willing to be lenient because you're learning, but you just failed to use my endearment. I wanted to be tender with you for our first night together but no, you went and ruined that! Open your legs!"

When Eve hesitated, Adara grabbed one of her breasts, twisting and squeezing it as she snarled, "Open your fucking leg, bitch!"

Eve felt her thighs part, hoping for the pain to stop but it didn't. A callous hand smacked her core repeatedly as she heard Adara speak, "This is mine now. Not yours, mine. Your entire body is my playground. That's all you are to me; a plaything. You're my piece of meat with holes to do with as I please. Why must you make me hurt you?"

"She has many valid points, plaything. You always seem to get yourself into trouble, time and time again. Lay there and take it, Eve. It's what you're good for, but even then, you'll still fail."

"Fuck off, asshole!" Eve growled at the demon, but then realized her outburst had once again got her into trouble. Adara glared at Eve with hatred as she bashed Eve's head into the wall several times, dazing her. Eve's whole world was spinning out of control as she felt a meaty hand roughly roll her over to where she now faced the wall.

"Fuck off, asshole? I don't think so, but I'll be fucking yours now." Adara pushed a pillow into Eve's face as she commanded, "Bite down, bitch, I'm going in dry!"

Eve barely had time to comprehend the order when a sharp pain assaulted her rectum, repeatedly stabbing its way inside her. Eve screamed as loudly as she could muster for help. The trauma she was getting from her cell mate got harder and more intense. Eve could barely comprehend the tirade coming from Adara. Her world seemed to push itself away, like a bubble in a vacuum void.

Eve barely felt the forced sodomy, just the pressure remaining as she somehow detached herself from her physical body. A commotion was taking place behind her as Eve felt the pressure alleviate from her backside. In an instant, Eve snapped painfully back into her body, screaming and crying against someone that was holding her.

"Fucking snitch!" Adara snarled as she spat at the guards, "I catch you; you are *dead*! You hear me, crazy girl!"

"Adara, I warned you about behaving yourself. Move her to cell block 3 with her friends."

"You can't do this!" Adara shrilled with terror, "My blood *will* be on your hands if you put me in *that* cell!"

"Not my concern. Perhaps you should have thought about that before you hurt this poor girl."

Eve could still hear her former cellmate screeching down the corridor as she laid down flat on her belly. Cold latex gloves prodded and probed her naked and battered form as people were talking amongst themselves. She knew that someone was speaking directly to her, asking questions, but Eve seemed to zone out, focusing on the dark figure outside the window. Eve noted from the shadowy stallion it sat on that it was the same entity from the bridge.

What was it and why is it following me, Eve pondered just as she passed out?

Chapter Three

Eve woke up alone in her cell, her body stiff and sore in multiple areas. She sat up, using the weighted blanket as a shield from the prying eyes of whomever was manning the camera. She felt her cheeks warm, knowing that that a recording of the sexual assault was filmed. People could access it and see everything. Eve wrapped the blanket around her body and gingerly walked over to the shelves.

Privacy was a luxury that Eve would never have for long. All she wanted to do was get dressed and hide under her cot, maybe draped the weighted blanket over the edge of the bed so none could see her exposed and vulnerable ever again.

Eve grabbed her scrub pants and managed to shimmy into them while holding up the blanket. She dropped the blanket with her back to her cell door and hurriedly put her scrub top on next. Eve couldn't help look out the window, wondering if she could get a better view of the horse-riding entity.

Nothing there, just car and foot traffic.

Eve snatched the weighted blanket off the floor and scurried into her cot just as the officer opened her cell door, followed closely by a woman in stylish business attire. Eve eyed the pair suspiciously, wondering what the two wanted from her.

"Eve Driskell, I'm Sergeant Davis and I brought with me -"

"Valerie Fisher," the attorney interrupted the Sergeant, stepping towards Eve, hand extended, "I've been assigned to you by the public defender's office on your behalf. It's nice to meet you, though I wish it were under circumstances."

Eve hesitated but didn't want to be rude to the only person that could get her out of the fire situation she faced, so she timidly offered her hand. The lawyer eyed the Sergeant as she shook hands, "If you could escort me and Miss Driskell to one of the consult rooms, I'd like some privacy with my client."

"Of course, but we will be monitoring the room closely since she's still on suicide watch. There is no audio, if you're concerned about that."

"Good, but I hope you have someone competent observing. I heard about what happened in this cell last night and saw the video evidence already. My faith in the department keeping Miss Driskell safe during her time of crisis is severely lacking."

"As the chief already told you, he's dealing with the mishaps that lead to last night's incident. Rest assured," the Sergeant looked into Eve's bloodshot eyes, "it won't happen again."

"If it does," Valerie eyed the officer with a steely gaze as she crossed her arms across her chest, "then I will hold the two of you personally responsible, as well as the department for failure to keep a high-profile prisoner safe from assault and sodomized in a cell that should have been only occupied by her."

The Sergeant stiffened as he walked over to the open cell door and stated, "I understand, now if you'll kindly follow me, I will lead the way to the consult room."

The lawyer offered a hand to Eve to assist her up. As she took the proffer hand, Eve felt a cold chill next to her. Eve glanced over, expecting to see the demon but saw something far worse.

Adara stood next to her.

Eve went pale as she stood, unwilling to let go of Valerie's hand. Eve's breathing quickened as she stuttered, not taking her gaze from the spectre, "C-can we g-go please?"

Valerie watched her clients fear and sudden terror, but saw nothing that could be triggering it. She pulled her hand from Eve's vise-like grip and grabbed her by the shoulders, turning her.

"Are you okay, Eve? You look as if you've seen a ghost."

"It's... it's Adara... she's... behind me!" Eve shrilled.

"Eve," the Sergeant impatiently admonished, "she's not in here. It's just you and Mrs. Fisher in here, now come along and follow me to the consult room."

"He's right, but he could learn a bit of tact, especially in my presence." She glared at the officer as they stepped out into the hall.

"Whatever, it's this way." The Sergeant marched ahead, not caring if they kept up.

Eve meandered beside Valerie, but kept looking over her shoulder. She sighed with relief, but it was a short respite. Adara materialized in front of her, giving Eve a murderous stare.

"This is all your fault, crazy girl! I wouldn't be like this if you would have done as you're told and kept that pretty little mouth of yours shut! If you thought last night was terrible, just wait, I have more in store for you, little bitch!"

Eve cringed, her body visibility shaking as a team of police officers raced by in a hurry. The lawyer shouted at the team, "Watch it, people are walking through here! What's going on?"

"Trouble in one of the cell blocks!" A female officer cried out.

"Hmm, I hope no one got hurt." Valerie commented to herself.

"Adara is dead, I'm sure of it..." Eve replied, her voice hollow.

Both Sergeant Davis and the lawyer stopped as they reached the consult room and turned to look at Eve.

"What makes you *think* that your assailant is dead?" Valerie asked, wondering if she heard about it from another inmate, but she dismissed this because Eve's been isolated from the general population.

"Because she's standing in front of me, threatening me."

The Sergeant rolled his eyes as he unlocked the door and sarcastically retorted, "First, it's a demon. Now there's a ghost! There's no such thing as either of those and if you ask me, your client sounds like she's trying to play the insanity card so she won't do any more jail time."

"Thankfully, nobody is asking you because it's beyond your pay grade to decide her sentence, that's up to Judge Goins. Now if you'll excuse us, my client and I have much to discuss."

The Sergeant almost spoke but thought better of it as he walked away. Valerie motioned for Eve to go into the private room and have a seat. She noticed that her client would flinch, like someone was yelling at her or maybe startled by something.

Eve nervously darted her wild eyes between the lawyer and the table. She bit her bottom lip, trying not to listen to the angry spectre to her right. It didn't help that her tormentor was sitting on the edge of the table, licking the lawyer's cheek.

"Eve," the lawyer started her assessment, "I know you have been through a lot last night and we can get into that later, if you wish. What I need is to hear your side of what occurred that led you to being on the St John's Bridge."

"I'm not sure where to begin," Eve sheepishly rubbed her left arm.

"*Start with how you work with a demon. I'm sure that she will believe you.*" The demon chuckled.

"Start with the events that led to you to be in your current situation." Valerie encouraged, "If more comes up, then feel free to share. Remember that I can't help you if I don't know the whole story."

"I-I hear the thoughts of people. Ever since I was fifteen years old. It was overwhelming and I thought I was going out of my mind. But in the last year and a half, I got them under control."

"How did you manage this? Are you currently on any medications for the voices at this time?" Valerie asked as she jotted down notes on her legal pad.

"I've been on meds..." Eve eyed her lawyer suspiciously, which gave Adara a chance to mock her.

"Crazy girl! You hear voices and tried to off yourself. Maybe you should have taken the whole bottle at once. Could have saved everyone some grief."

"I've said as much Adara, but Eve never listens. Perhaps you can help me with changing her

stubborn attitude. I loved your lesson you gave Eve last night, as crude as it was. You can do better."

"What-what are you? How do you know my name?" Adara asked as she examined Eve's tormentor.

"So, you're currently *not* in any medications at this time? " The lawyer asked.

"No ma'am, nothing works. So, I stopped taking them. I can block all the thoughts out, save one."

"Which one is that?"

"Say it, Eve. Tell the pretty lady who's your master." The demon goaded, "We haven't got all day. The nut house is waiting for you to check in."

Eve gulped as she hung her head in shame, "The demon. He's the reason why I am here."

Valerie's hand froze mid stroke. She eyed her client, wondering if she truly believed this or if what the Sergeant said earlier is closer to the truth.

"A demon?!" Adara squealed, "You mean that crazy girl was really hearing you? But-"

"Yes, I'm quite real and seeing as you're a ghost means you can see and hear me too. I was in the cell, watching you put Eve through Hell. I enjoyed watching your passing in cell block 3, most unfortunate."

Adara wailed in fear as she left the room, making the sign of the cross with her ethereal fingers as the demon laughed. Eve covered her ears to block it out, but to no avail.

"Are you hearing this *demon* of yours right now?" The lawyer asked, studying her fidgety client.

Eve slowly nodded, "And I can see it too."

"When you see and hear it, what exactly occurs?"

"It gets me into trouble," Eve answered as she watched the demon standing behind her lawyer, "I see it hurting people and I try to stop it, but my actions get construed as an attack. It can project images to me that aren't happening and for some reason, I can't help myself. I try to protect others, but it always backfires, which is why I've been in and out of hospitals."

"Is this demon doing anything currently?"

Eve watched her tormentor grab a handfuls of the lawyer's blouse and rip it open, causing buttons to fly everywhere. It's sickly clawed hands groped Valerie's ample breasts as it slid its slimy tongue anywhere it could.

Eve grimaced as she averted her eyes in disgust, "I'd rather not say, it's being a disgusting pig."

"Very well, tell me about the day you tried to kill yourself." Valerie reached out and squeezed Eve's hand, "I know that may be difficult to talk about, but I'm going to need you to try for me."

"I'm pretty much destitute. I lost yet another job and I'm fixing to get evicted from my apartment. I didn't want to end up in a homeless shelter or on the streets, not again. Things got to be too much so I drove to the bridge. I didn't intend to park my car on the bridge. I was going to take an old side road that led to the river and drive straight into it, but that got bungled."

"How so?"

Eve let out a long sigh, "The demon. It messed with my head, arguing and taunting me to the point where I got distracted and before I knew it, I was on the bridge. I tried to turn around and leave, but traffic was too thick and I ended up blocking people. I was so distraught...I got out of the car and made my way to the edge."

"Oh sure," the demon huffed, *"blame me for your piss poor driving. I'm not the one who missed a massive river with a car. You're weak and pathetic."*

"Fuck off, I'm not weak or pathetic!" Eve snapped as she stood up, ready to fight the demon.

"Eve!" Valerie warned, but was ready to run out the door, "please control your temper. Remember that the guards are watching and you may get unwillingly escorted back to your cell."

"You don't understand," Eve slumped down in her chair, tears painfully threatened to unleash with her frustration, "he mocks and demeans me every waking moment of every day. I wish that I could rip out his sickly tongue and shove it down its throat."

"I see," the lawyer stated flatly, hoping that her client wouldn't become aggressive as she inquired further. An officer stood at the door, ready to come in, but Valerie quickly held up a hand. She composed herself and asked, "Now tell me why you bit the EMT worker after you were talked down from the ledge?"

Eve blushed and turned her head, "The demon was in full mental abuse mode because I didn't kill myself and he got on my last nerve. He got in my face and since I was being restrained, I did the only logical move: I bit off his nose...only it wasn't the demon my teeth sank into..."

"So, this demon made you bite her, the EMT?" When Eve nodded slowly, Valerie continued, "Do you want to talk about what happened last night?"

Eve stoically shrugged her shoulders, "Adara bullied me, beat me, humiliated and..." she closed her eyes and the tears cascaded unchecked, "raped me. What more is there to say, other than she can't hurt me ever again?"

"Because you believe that she's dead, but now can see her as a ghost? Are you still seeing her?" Valerie repeatedly tapped her pen, cynically eyeing Eve.

"No, she freaked out when she saw the demon and ran off," Eve giggled but then she grew silent, her mood melancholic as she added, "but I suppose Adara will come back to torment me. She blames me for her death because I was screaming last night."

Valerie gathered her things as she stood up and motioned to the officer to come in as she spoke, "I believe that I've heard enough and I will go over my notes to come up with a plan to get you the help you deserve. Judge Goins will see you in a few days and we will know more after her ruling."

As Eve stepped out into the hall and was escorted back to her cell. The lawyer noticed a body being taken out on a gurney. The blanket obscured the body, but blood was soaking through in spots. Valerie caught the chief of precinct and asked, "May I ask, was that an inmate or one of yours?"

The chief eyed her for a moment and then replied, "An inmate. It should make your client rest easier to know that Adara Miller won't trouble her ever again."

"Adara's dead?" Valerie paled as she recalled what Eve told her, "When did it happen?"

"I'd say about the time you met with your client in her cell."

Valerie felt overwhelmed so she curtly nodded to the chief and marched out of the building to her car. As she got into her car, she pressed the ignition button and glanced back at the police station, questions gnawing at her. Is Eve Driskell mentally ill or is she truly seeing and hearing things that only she can perceive?

Chapter Four

Several days later, Eve patiently sat on a bench, waiting for her turn to speak with the judge. From what she learned from her lawyer; Eve had a feeling that today wouldn't go well. It all hinged on Judge Goins and her evaluation of the case. Eve didn't want to go back to jail but also, she didn't want to get court ordered to the state hospital either.

Unfortunately, even if the judge somehow miraculously released her, Eve had no place to live. She got word from her landlord that she was no longer a tenant and all her belongings had been sold or discarded. This felt like a nightmare, one that seemed to never end. Eve hunched over to cry, being in shackles made it difficult to cover her face. It didn't help that her tormentor was crouched on the wall behind her, adding additional salt onto her wounds.

"Save the tears for the judge, Eve. They might win her over, but I highly doubt it. You are better off in jail because nobody else will have you. Certainly not your landlord. Great job at keeping a roof over your pathetic head."

"Shut up and leave me alone, for once!" Eve growled over her shoulder, "God, get a life or something. Don't you have demonic things to do?"

"*I do,*" the demon mocked, "*it involves you. I have to tell you what's going on because you are incapable of independent thought. I mean, how else do you explain your current situation?*"

"Easy, this is all *your* fault!" Eve retorted but then noticed that the other inmates and guards were eyeing her. Some snickered while others eyed her with contempt. Eve's cheeks heated as she heard the demon chuckling, knowing full well that it wanted her to yell at it in front of everyone. It was really good at doing that, easily having Eve make a fool of herself.

"*My fault? How is all this my fault? I'm not the one who bit that poor lady on the bridge. I'm not the one who can't keep a job or a home. I'm not the one that makes the poor decisions, now am I? I'm just an observer and I see you for what you truly are, Eve.*"

"And what am I?" Eve inquired but already knew the answer.

"*You are a waste of oxygen and not worth anyone's time because you're broken and can't be fixed. You're as beautiful as a salted slug with brains to match. If I had any sense, I would leave you to your own devices.*"

"Then run off and amuse yourself elsewhere. I think you've done enough damage here."

The demon got in Eve's face, grabbing her jaw forcefully, causing pinpricks of blood to appear from its sickly claws. It stared her down as it coldly spoke with authority, "*I never give up on what's mine. You are my plaything and as such, I can do whatever I please to you. You may have psychic gifts, but they are paltry at best. You are too weak to use them and scared of your own shadow and that makes you special to no one. Don't think that you can tell me what to do because nothing you can do can affect me. You will know your place, child, and who is the master in our relationship.*"

The door to the courtroom opened at that moment, the bailiff called out, "Eve Driskell!"

The demon released her jaw and stood ominous before Eve as she stood up to shuffle her way into the courtroom as she muttered, "Asshole!"

It was a small room, just a bench for the judge to preside over each hearing with the state and American flag in the backdrop. Two long dark wood tables, one for the district attorney and the other had Valerie seated, waiting for her. The room was sparsely decorated, the walls were egg white and had trimming the same style as the other wooden furniture. As the judge entered the courtroom, the demon chuckled as it mocked, "*Time to make a great first impression so everyone will remember you. The way is to make an ass of yourself so why not do it now?*"

Eve gasped as she felt her orange scrub pants get yanked down to her ankles and forcefully shoved into the district attorney's table. All the court officials gasped, not fully understanding what just happened and how Eve managed this. Eve clenched her jaw as her eyes shut tightly, not wanting to see the mortified looks as her pale toned ass was on display for all to witness.

"Oh dear. Somebody forgot about the dress code for court." The demon tsked, *"You're so stupid that you forgot that I rule over your life entirely."*

She felt hands grabbing to stand her upright as someone shimmied her scrub pants back up her body. As she was being escorted to her seat, Eve heard a female voice bark out, "Ms. Driskell, I expect better conduct in my courtroom. I hope that there won't be any further disrespectful behavior."

"No, your honor," Eve meekly replied, not daring to look at the judge.

"I will ensure that Eve Driskell shows more restraint," Valerie pleaded, trying to placate the judge, "you have my word, your honor."

"See to it, Mrs. Fisher. I don't know how your client managed it, but any more stunts like that will not be tolerated and I *will* fine her for contempt of court."

"That's the spirit, Eve!" the demon purred next to Eve's ear, *"You managed to get on the judge's good side by showing off your backside.*

Your talent for making a good impression exceeds my expectations, as always!"

Eve looked at her lawyer and whispered, "I'm sorry, but that wasn't my doing."

"Never mind that, let's hope it doesn't occur again." Mrs. Fisher replied as she motioned for Eve to stand as the bailiff called for the court to be in session. Eve glanced down and saw the demon sprawled out on her table with a mocking grin, *"I'm the one in charge, know this."*

Eve barely nodded in agreement, not wanting her tormentor do something more dramatic. The demon chuckled as it pawed at her, trying to get a rise out of Eve. The demon pouted as Eve sat down unfazed. Judge Goins looked at the prosecutor and asked, "Does the State wish to make it's opening statement?"

"Yes, your honor," a youthful male lawyer replied as he stood in his custom-tailored gray suit, "The facts of this case speaks volumes about Ms. Driskell. Her mental health is in decline and has exhibited behavior that is both detrimental to herself and those around her. Examples of this are as follows: a blatant disregard for the lives of others attempting to cross the St John's Bridge; her attempted suicide; assaulting a first responder by biting her, claiming that she was 'a demon'. This shows just how much of a danger Ms. Driskell is to the public and herself. The defendant needs to stand trial for her actions. Thank you, your honor."

"Noted, Does the defense have a statement to give for these charges?"

"Yes, honor." Valerie stood up and glanced down at her client, "The defense can't dispute the State's case against my client, but if the State wants to have a criminal trial, then Ms. Driskell needs to be able to aid and assist in her trial. As the State already alluded to, my client's mental health is in an already fragile state. Being incarcerated hasn't helped, if anything, it's added more trauma. We request that she be placed at the Oregon State Hospital for evaluation under the Oregon Stature 161.370."

Eve panicked as she looked at her lawyer, wondering why she wanted to send her to the state hospital. Judge Goins looked at Eve and asked, "Ms. Driskell, is there something you wish to say on your behalf?"

"Oh, this should be good. How I wish I had popcorn for my front row seat to disaster."

"Yes, your honor! Why must I get sent to the state hospital? The demon has been causing all of the problems! It torments me day and night. Even now, it's laying here, mocking me. It was the demon that made me…" Eve took a deep breath as the demon chuckled with anticipation, "bare all in your court. Either get me a priest to perform an exorcism or just shoot me dead. I'm tired of the Hell I'm in, please make something good happen for me."

"Ms. Driskell, the court has heard your pleas and I'm sympathetic to your plight. I truly am," Judge Goins empathetically said, "which is why I must, in good conscience, recommend you be transferred to the Oregon State Hospital for treatment and evaluation to stand trial. I pray that you get the much needed therapy for your mental health, but also for the trauma you've endured recently. Maybe the doctors there can get you on the medication regime that will stop the voice of this demon. If there are no further objections?"

When both sides agreed, Judge Goins added, "This case will reconvene if and when Ms. Eve Driskell is able to aid and assist in her defense in accordance with Oregon Stature 161.370."

Eve stood in shock as officers escorted her out of the courtroom. Tears trickled down her cheeks as her lawyer stepped up beside her, trying to comfort her, "I know that this isn't the outcome you hoped for, but at least you won't be staying in that terrible jail."

"Nothing matters anymore," Eve spoke as if she were somewhere distant and numb, "my suffering will follow me no matter where I go. Why couldn't they just let me die..."

Chapter Five

The road was slick from the rain and snow mixture that the clouds above was unleashing today. Eve sat quietly on the bench seat as she was being transferred to the state hospital. Eve had never been there before but heard too many stories that filled her with trepidation.

She glanced out the window, not sure why, just to pass the time. Something would catch her attention, just out of her peripheral vision. Eve barely registered it at times but when she did, she wondered if it was the shadowy figure on horseback.

Whatever it was, it managed to keep pace with the transport bus and remain stealthily concealed. Eve sighed, wishing that everything and everyone in the world would leave her be, but that was a fairy tale that would never come to pass. Next to her sat another prisoner. She had long red hair with the sides shaved underneath the fiery mane. Both her arms were covered with tattoos of skulls and other images that represented death. She had an old scar that ran down the side of her left cheek but it didn't detract from her beauty. The woman could have been in her late thirties but Eve couldn't be sure.

"So, Eve," the woman spoke calmly, "you ready for a stent in the state hospital?"

Eve's eyes widened, "How do you know my name? Have we met before?"

"No, but I *do* know who you are. You were once a cellmate with Adara."

As soon as the woman said Adara's name, Eve tensed up and flinched. She felt a hand curl around her hand, she squeezed it and added, "Don't worry, kid. I took care of that fat pig personally. You won't be bothered by her anymore."

Eve closed her eyes, "If only that were true..."

"Before she got thrown in my cellblock, I was awoken by someone screaming. I assume that was you. The bitch dropped your name as the guards pushed her in with my crew. Would it please you to know that she pissed herself when she saw me?"

Eve gulped as she whispered, ashamed that her cry for help led to Adara's demise, "Why are you telling me this, you don't know me?"

"True, but I never liked Adara and her bullying attitude. You granted me the opportunity to deal with her permanently and for that, I thank you."

"And because I squealed, she's dead and it's all my fault," Eve let the tears flow. Her tormentor wasn't around currently, but she knew he would agree with this. "And now I will be next to die because-"

"Whoa, hold up Eve!" The redheaded prisoner interrupted, "Who's threatening you? You tell me right now and I *will* see that they never touch you."

"No one has but," Eve gasped, trying to speak during her emotional breakdown, "Adara said it would happen if I squealed. Just let me die, I'm not worth it."

"That *pig* did a number on you in such a short time." The woman spat on the floor board. She draped a comforting arm around

Eve's quivering body, "You're not in jail anymore and no one else is coming after you. You sound like you need a friend and I'd like to be friends with you Eve, if you'll let me."

"Friends never stick around for long, so why bother with me, um what's your name?"

"I go by Red Jayne, but you can just call me Jayne or Red, whichever you prefer. Why would I leave you? What makes you so certain that I would abandon you like your other supposed 'friends'?"

"Isn't it obvious," Eve motioned to the front of the vehicle, "I'm being taken to the hospital because I'm weird and freak people out because of the stuff I say and the...things I see."

Jayne smirked, "If you haven't noticed, it's my destination as well. It's not so bad, just mind your own business, do your treatment, behave, and you will do fine."

"Easier said than done," Eve slumped her shoulders, shaking her head in defeat, "all I do is get into trouble and make things worse for myself and those around me. Why wouldn't they let me die?"

"I will say this much: I've been through a lot and seen some fucked up shit in my life so when I say that I got your back, I mean it. No matter how batshit crazy you go, I'm here for you."

Eve shrugged her shoulders slightly, "You say that now, but once you see me battling my personal demon, you will leave. Everyone does."

"I understand, we all have our own personal demons to deal with, but -"

"You don't understand," Eve interrupted, hoping to push Jayne away now, before her tormentor returns from wherever it goes off to, "I'm talking about a demon. Not some negative crap spewing around in my brain. A demonic entity that relishes in making my life a living hell."

Red Jayne pulled her arm off Eve, confusion warred across her visage. Eve felt that she did her job and alienated this woman to the point of going speechless. After a few minutes had silently passed, Jayne whispered, "Is it here with you, right now?"

"*Do tell the red-mane fool that I'm always here with you. Did you really believe that you were alone?*" The demon chuckled as it perched itself on the top of the bench seat in front of Eve.

"Yes, it is," Eve pointed at it, knowing full well that her new *friend* wouldn't see it, as she kept her head hung low in shame. Jayne eyed the bench seat for a moment and then stated, "Get lost, asshole! Eve doesn't need you around her anymore. And another thing, wipe that idiotic smirk off your face."

Eve quickly looked up and caught the demon smirking as it observed Red Jayne, seemingly amused by her proclamation. He glanced over at Eve with a malicious glint in its eyes.

"*She doesn't see me, it's all a front for your benefit,*" the demon commented as it slid its hand onto Jayne's body, groping one of her breasts, causing her to shiver slightly, "*That being said, I will have some enjoyment with this one. I do hope that you two are roommates, I want you to see everything. She has a strange power within her that I'm dying to exploit."*

Before Eve could warn her of the demon's threat, Jayne did something that took both her and the demon by surprise. Jayne reached out and grabbed the demon by its muscular forearm and retched it away from her body but didn't let go. The shock on the demon's visage was enough to give Eve pause, wondering how Red Jayne accomplished this feat.

"I don't appreciate non-consensual pawing done by people, let alone a filthy demon." Jayne's grip tightened as Eve's tormentor attempted to free itself. With a quick twist of her wrist, Jayne managed to break the inhuman creature's forearm like it was a stick. The demon howled a blood curdling scream, causing Eve to cover her ears.

"Let that be a lesson to you, demon." Jayne coldly spoke as she pulled the entity to her face, "Eve is *mine*, not yours. If I hear from you again, I won't be as merciful as I am right now. Take a hike!"

Jayne pushed the demon back forcefully, causing it to tumble out of the vehicle as it let out a profanity laced oath. Eve gazed at Jayne in rapt awe, wanting to know if what she just witnessed really happened.

"How did you do that?" Eve barely squeaked out.

Red Jayne turned to look at her and said, "It's something that I can do. Something that I've done my whole life."

"Can," Eve hesitated, but her excitement pushed her to ask, "can you teach me to do what you just did?"

"I might be willing to but," Jayne turned to Eve and grazed her fingers across her jawline, "there's a price to be paid. I don't do this sort of thing for free."

"Do you want me here or somewhere else then? I'm yours to do as you please. I want to know how to fight like you do." Eve sadly asked, feeling like she was selling her body.

Red Jayne gasped, "What? No! As lovely as sex with you would be, that's not what I'm referring to. Man, Adara really did a number on you. My price is being honest with me. If I ask you a question, you *must* tell me the truth."

"Oh," Eve rubbed her arm as her cheeks flushed, "that sounds fair."

"Good," Jayne stated as the van turned right on Center Street, "now answer me this: do you have any *gifts*?"

"Um," Eve shifted uncomfortably, "what do you mean by gifts?"

"You know what I mean, Eve." Jayne eyed her, "You just witnessed what I did to your demon. What abilities do you have?"

"I-I hear the thoughts of the people around me. Does that count?"

"Yes, it does," Jayne smiled, "is it constant or can you block it out?"

"In the beginning, I was bombarded by so many voices that I thought I was going insane. I called for help, anything to make it stop."

"And that's where your demonic friend came into play, right?"

Eve looked down at the floorboard, nodding her head in shame, "He promised to teach me how to harness my gift as long as I was his student and sought help from no one else. Now, he spends his time torturing me and causing a lot of grief in the process. There's nothing I can do about him. I guess I deserve it."

"Damn right, you deserve it," Jayne quickly snapped, "Magic always comes with a price and you are paying for it right now. That's what you get for dealing with a demon. Your ignorance is your ultimate downfall, so you need to learn more from others, like myself. But I'm not sure if you can mentally handle it."

Eve shrugged her shoulders, "You're probably right. I did try to end my life and yet, the demon prevented it and used it as another chance to humiliate and mock me. If you want to help me, you could break my neck. I won't fight back."

"And there lies the problem with you. No fight. You'd rather give up than take a stand against your demon or anyone else for that matter." Jayne roughly caressed Eve's back, "You do have spine. Now use your backbone for once and stand up for yourself. I'm not going to fight your battles for you while you sit back and cry."

"Easy for you to say," Eve hissed indignantly, "you know nothing about what I've gone through my whole life! I'm so low right now that death is a welcoming sight. Hell, I'm going to be locked up in the state hospital. It doesn't get much worse than that."

"I don't care about your pathetic life story or shortcomings, Eve," Jayne coldly answered as the van pulled into the state hospital parking lot, "Everyone has those, but they don't define who we are. You learn and grow or wallow in your past failures and become stagnant. Choose now, little girl, because I'm not wasting my time on a lost cause."

"If you teach me what I need to know, I will listen, but frankly, I may be a lost cause."

"More like misguided," Jayne corrected her, "I expect you will take this seriously, considering what the alternative is for you and what's about to happen."

"I promise you that I will do my best, Jayne. Let's shake in agreement," Eve put her hand out to shake hands, but Jayne took it and pulled her towards her. She roughly pressed her lips against Eve's soft lips, surprising her, and then snaked her tongue into her mouth. Eve obliged by opening her mouth so her new teacher could explore, which caused Jayne to giggle slightly.

She pulled away from Eve, licking her lips with a devilish smile, "I don't shake hands. I seal all my deals with a kiss. It's my way of gauging if you're being honest with me or holding back on the deal. Don't fret, you passed."

Eve's cheeks redden slightly as the van pulled up to a metal garage bay door. One of the transport officers got out and pressed the button on the intercom while his partner sat behind the wheel, tapping on it repetitively because his window wouldn't roll down.

"Have you been in here before," Eve whispered, feeling a sense of dread as the garage bay door slowly rolled up.

"Several times. Have you?"

"I've been committed to other institutions, just not this one."

Jayne nodded as the van pulled forward into the garage, "It's not a bad place, but just be warned, since you can obviously see a demon, you will see other strange things lurking around, other than the patients and staff."

"Wonderful," Eve muttered weakly, wishing that she had better ways to protect herself, like Jayne.

The side door opened as the officer motioned for the two women to disembark. Jayne stood, smirking as she shambled her way to the door. As Eve stood up to get out, her knees trembled and her gait unsteady from her shackles. She gripped each seat as she walked by like a lifeline as she stumbled awkwardly towards the waiting hand of the deputy.

Jayne made it look effortlessly to walk in these, Eve thought as she tentatively stepped out onto the concrete floor. The deputy held her by her elbow as he escorted her to stand by the wall.

"Wait here for your turn," the officer stated as he released her. He stood next to her, towering over Eve by a foot. She heard water running from somewhere beyond the gray metal door and watched the other cop talking to several people that work here. They were signing forms when all of a sudden, someone blurted out, "Smile!"

Eve was momentarily blinded and disoriented from the flash, "Huh, what was that?"

"Sorry about that," the cheerful man stated, "We need a picture of you for your ID and for your file. Didn't mean to blind you."

Two female staff stepped out into the garage and motioned for Eve, "We're ready for her."

The deputy stepped in front of Eve, eyeing her as he unlocked her wrist shackles, and commanded, "Don't try anything stupid."

Eve meekly nodded as she rubbed her wrists, "There's nothing I can do."

"Not what I've heard," the towering cop replied as he released her feet. He unhooked the chain around her waist and added, "Behave yourself. These people are here to help you. I hope you get the help you need, Ms. Driskell."

She walked over to the two female staff as both deputies got back into the transport van.

"Eve Driskell?" The older of the two asked. She nodded and was asked, "My name is Meghan and this Claire. We will be helping you with your admission. What size clothes do you wear?"

"Medium."

Meghan curtly nodded, motioning for Eve, "Good. If you can step through here, Claire and I will assist you in the shower."

Eve nervously bit her bottom lip as she stepped inside the facility. As the door closed behind her, Eve heard the van start up and pull out of the garage. She took a deep breath as Claire handed her several towels, a small cup of liquid soap. Meghan opened a side door which led to a small room that had a toilet, a sink with a push button, and a showerhead on the wall that resembled a metal door stop.

It too, had a push button which Claire explained, "The shower is turned on by pressing this button. Same goes for the sink. It's only on for a short time so you'll have to press it as you shower. The bathroom in your room is set up like this, minus the window over there. We will be monitoring you so you can shower with some privacy. We'll have a fresh set of state issue clothes once you finish up."

"What do I do with these?" Eve asked as tugged on her orange jail scrubs.

"Put them by the sink and we will take care of them. You won't be needing them while you're here. Understand?"

Eve nodded as the hospital staff exited the tiny bathroom. She couldn't see the women through the window, but could tell that they were there. She kicked off her shoes as she turned away from the window and tugged her scrub top off and carefully pulled her pants down.

Will this humiliation ever end?

She bundled up her clothes and placed them on the small counter space. Eve stepped under the shower head, pressed the button, and was greeted by icy cold water. She yelped as she skidded away from it as a voice on an intercom spoke, "Just let it run. It will eventually heat up."

Eve reached out with her hand to gauge the water temperature. It wasn't as cold but she didn't like being this exposed, so she gritted her teeth and stepped under the oddly cascading water. She lathered a wash rag with the liquid soap and vigorously scrubbed her body. Tears streamed down her face, masked by the shower.

Suddenly the water stopped, causing Eve to nervously jump. Meghan spoke over the intercom, "Just press the button, Eve. It's on a timer to shut off."

Eve blindly fondled the wall, hunting for the button, her eyes covered in soap. Her hand brushed against a cold metal knob which could only be the water button. She pressed it and more water sprung out. After five minutes, Eve finished up and grabbed a towel. She sat down on the metal toilet to dry off.

The door opened and Claire stepped inside with a small bundle of clothes and a pair of black rubber sandals. She placed them on the counter and took Eve's clothes with her as she stated, "When you're done and dressed, we will take you to the ward."

Eve nodded as she clutched her towel tightly to her body. She felt so ashamed, wishing that she had the courage to jump off the bridge. As if thinking of that night, right on cue, her tormentor appeared on the wall beside her.

I see that you've taken to performing voyeuristic shows for the nice people here. Dance to their delight.

Eve ignored him as she stood up to get dressed, but the demon violently snatched her towel out of her hands and he mocked, "*Stop being a tease and show the men beyond the wall your disgusting flesh.*"

"There's no men out there," Eve hissed under her breath as she quickly got dressed, but her voice echoed in the small bathroom, "It's just Meghan and Claire watching. I'm pretty sure it's a rule for female staff to assist female patients."

"Rules are meant to be broken. Since when have rules or the law, for that matter, ever weighed in your favor?"

Eve put on a pair of gray sweatpants that had no drawstring and gray sweatshirt. As she slipped into the black rubber sandals, the door was held open for her. Meghan stuck beside her as Claire led the way. She used her badge to unlock each door that crossed their winding path.

The floor was made of concrete and the walls were an off-white color. Everything about this place seemed dreary and depressing to Eve. Shadows danced and flickered just out of her peripheral vision, though her escorts didn't notice.

Maybe they're used to it?

Eve looked up and saw the word *Lighthouse* just above a short hallway. They stopped next to an elevator, which Meghan had to scan her badge before it would open. As the doors opened, Claire motioned for Eve to enter. She kept her head down as she stepped inside, making her way to the back meekly.

"You'll be staying on Lighthouse 3. It's an all female unit. One of the only ones in the hospital," Meghan explained as the elevator slowly, "There're several co-ed units, but for now, you will be with us."

"For how long?" Eve squeaked out.

"It all depends on you, Eve," Claire answered as the elevator door opened, "Since you're here as a .370, your stay could be short. We're here to help you learn legal skills so you can aid and assist in your legal case."

Claire used her badge on the black electronic lock and held open the door. Eve shuffled onto the unit. It felt cold and uninviting, all the doors that they passed down the long corridor were metal.

"*The perfect tomb for you, little girl,*" her tormentor mocked.

"Fuck off," Eve hissed under her breath.

She was shown the entire unit, which consisted of two more long halls, each having the same number of patient rooms, a laundry room, and a phone that had a bench inlaid into the wall. At the junction where these halls veered from each other, two identical rooms sat that were connected by a free swinging door on the wall and an air court that overlooked the outside world through black steel cage barriers.

Opposite of the day rooms sat a small cubicle with thick plexiglass encasing it that staff sat in to monitor the ward, aptly referred to as "The Bubble". Two larger activity rooms flanked it and we're used to eat meals and snacks, as well as for playing games and passing the time. Straight across from The Bubble was a consult room, where patients could make private phone calls to their lawyer and meet with their treatment team.

Meghan unlocked the consult room and led Eve inside. There wasn't anything special about the room; a long table with chairs surrounding every side of it and a wooden locked cabinet that had a landline phone inside. Paperwork sat upon the table, along with a guy that Eve didn't recognize.

"Eve Driskell," the man asked as he looked at her over the metal rims of his glasses. She nodded as he stood up and pulled out a chair for her to sit on. "Take a seat. We have a lot of paperwork to go over and sign."

My life is nothing more than a large file of legal and medical documents.

"See? You should've jumped when you had the chance but you couldn't accomplish that. Foolish girl."

After several hours of questions about her health and history from the man, as well as a doctor and a social worker, Eve felt drained. She barely registered the barbs that her tormentor cast at her. She roamed the unit, not wanting to interact with any of her peers. Everywhere she went, Meghan followed closely by for safety reasons because of her "history", as the doctor put it.

Chapter Six

Eve's routine consisted, for the first few weeks of being at the hospital, of getting up, eating her meals, taking her medication, and going to Treatment Mall for leisure time in the morning and legal skills learning in the afternoon. At least she got to see Jayne in the morning, though she was on a different unit in the Harbors stack. On a daily basis, Eve would end up in restraints, claiming a demon was hurting someone. It was her reason behind each of her assaultive behavior. In between all this, Eve paced the unit or hung out in her room, crying. She tried to not look around as she paced, the otherworldly entities seemed abundant here, just as Jayne said.

Eve no longer cared about the outside world. She was resigned that her life would be spent in this dismal place. Eve sat on her bed, which was nothing more than a plastic, one-piece bed frame bolted to the floor with a foam mattress, encased in faux leather for easy sterilization. Every piece of furniture in her room was bolted down to the concrete flooring and walls.

There was a writing desk that sat under a long window that was flanked by shelves that reminded Eve of children's cubby holes like she had in Kindergarten for her clothing and other approved items. She had her own "private" bathroom with a shower that operated like the one she had to use during her admission into the hospital.

Due to Eve's unpredictable history, staff had to observe her whenever she used the restroom. Eve felt like the eyes of everyone was constantly on her, both physically and otherworldly.

Eve looked up at the staff that was assigned to her for the hour. The guy was cute and young, holding a well-worn manilla folder with doodles on each side. He wore black jeans and a plain red shirt with a badge that dangled from a lanyard around his neck. Eve wished that she could see the rest of his face. With the flu pandemic, everyone that worked at the hospital had to wear face masks as a precaution and to keep this year's deadly flu strain from infecting the patients.

Eve noticed that her psychic gift kept coming to the forefront, allowing her to hear the private thoughts of everyone around her. No matter what she tried or what new drugs that the doctor of her ward prescribed, nothing helped. She pleaded with her tormentor for guidance, but he became more abusive.

Despite this, Eve was able to hear his thoughts and wondered if that was the reason that the demon was becoming increasingly cross with her. His thoughts surprised her, the demon seemed to have similar thoughts and insecurities as her and other people. Eve stood up, as did her current staff, and said, "May I go out on the air court for some fresh air, please?"

"Sure, Eve. Let me move my chair first." The tech replied. She nodded as he put the hard-plastic chair just inside her room. Eve stepped out and paused, seeing shadowy figures fluttering in and out of the walls. She gulped as she slowly walked down the hall, keeping her eyes cast down.

She heard the tech next to her chuckled to himself, her gift of hearing other people's thoughts made it apparent what was so humorous.

"Why are they called hallways here in this place, when psychopaths seems more of an appropriate name?"

Eve did her best to stifle a giggle, but it escaped her lips. She glanced over at her escort and saw that he was watching her intently.

"What's so funny, Ms. Driskell?"

She nervously nibbled on her bottom lip, "Nothing."

The tech eyed her with a wry smile, Eve heard his mental commentary again, *"I get it. It's an inside joke that I wouldn't understand."*

Eve sighed as they entered the day room, "So true."

Her psychic gift seemed to be getting worse, more pronounced. Eve was used to focusing on hearing other people's thoughts, but lately those thoughts were coming to her unabated. Eve had a hell of a time around the other patients, especially the ones that were schizophrenic or in a manic episode. Her tormentor didn't seem bothered by this new development.

The demon delighted in her suffering, mocking her inability to control it by saying, *"It's your own fault that you're like this now. So pathetic. So weak. Frankly, I can't think of a better torture for you than what you're doing to yourself. Deep down, Eve, you know that you deserve it."*

Eve couldn't find any rational reason to think otherwise, the demon knew her better than she knew herself. The day room consisted of several heavy-duty plastic chairs, a round table and swinging door that led to another day room. A large wooden cabinet housed a TV behind plexiglass with a DVD player on the covered shelf below.

Eve walked to the door that led to the air court, avoiding the weary looks from the other female patients. The tech pushed the door open, holding it for Eve. She stepped out on the air court, which was encased in a solid metal mesh that let in a cool breeze.

She sat down on a heavy-duty plastic rocking chair. The view wasn't spectacular, the parking lot was packed with a plethora of vehicles and an open field. To her right, the ballfield sat and further away, was the state penitentiary. In the field, Eve caught sight of the shadowy figure on horseback. The little psychic wondered if this entity was here for her. It seemed to follow her everywhere she went since the night at the bridge.

She closed her eyes and rocked in place. Her peace was short lived as she heard the voice of her tormentor. The demon hung onto the metal mesh, mocking the little psychic, *"Such a marvelous view, don't you think? It's too bad that you'll never know freedom."*

"Go away," Eve muttered under her breath.

"Did you say something, Eve?" The tech asked as he eyed her.

"I suggest that you end your life, but we both know that you can't even accomplish that feat. Pathetic girl!"

Eve jumped up, surprising the male tech next to her. She growled as she ran at the demon, her fist clenched. She punched at the demon, but her fist connected with the metal mesh screen. She yelped as her tormentor cackled. Her tech called out to Eve as she kept punching the metal screen, "Eve, stop! Staff!"

Eve watched the demon move over to her personal staff. It stood there in front of the man, clawing at his chest. He winced as he put his hands up, trying to calm down Eve. The demon grinned, *"Isn't this one a cutie? You two would make a lovely couple, but we both know that you will destroy his heart. No one can love you, Eve. Want to see his heart?"*

Eve's eyes widened as her tormentor used its magic, making her 'see' him rip out the tech's heart. The little psychic vehemently spat, "I'll fucking kill you for that!"

"Oh shit!" He shouted as Eve charged at him. Her fists assailed the tech's face as the demon cackled. More staff spilled into the air court, grabbing Eve by her arms and pulled her out as her tech fell down. Eve thrashed around, trying to free herself, when one of the nurses ordered, "Take her to the floor! Someone grabbed the Stryker stretcher!"

Eve was sprawled out on the hard floor; her arms were stretched out as the techs leaned their weight on them. She felt hands grasp her ankles and more weight on her calves.

"You don't understand," Eve cried out as tears streamed down her face, "I'm trying to save his life!"

The demon got in Eve's peripheral vision, smirking as he clicked his tongue, "*You certainly did save his life. Poor Derek is going to the hospital. Your failure is on full display, as usual. You must be proud of yourself, Eve.*"

Eve buried her face in the floor, snot dripping from her nose as she felt the restraints snuggly pressed on her ankles and wrists. She heard a patient cry out, "I love soccer, bitch!"

Eve heard feet stomping and felt the tip of a shoe connect with her left temple. The surrounding staff yelled as they chased after the other patient as she laughed down the hallway. Eve's head lulled as her body was rolled over onto an orange backboard. Safety belts were snapped over her as a nurse leaned down to examine Eve.

The little psychic was dazed, her ears rang and she had difficulty focusing on the different questions from the nurse next to her. Mentally, she kept hearing a strange phrase from all those around her. It's the same one that kept repeating in the minds of both the patients and staff.

"Prepare...The Reset is coming..."

Eve noticed that her body was lifted up in the air and then placed on the Stryker stretcher. More safety belts were fastened across her little body. As she was pushed out of the day room down the hall, Eve opened her eyes and saw the demon sitting on her legs. She wasn't sure if it was the kick to the head playing tricks on her mind, but she could've sworn that her tormentor had a look of concern. Fear?

Eve wondered what would cause a demon to experience pure terror? It looked down at her and sneered as the stretcher was pushed into a small room with a bed in the middle of it. The staff kept talking to each other as they coordinated together to move Eve safety to the bed.

"*Stop eavesdropping in my head, child. It's quite rude.*" The demon chided.

"Maybe you can teach me to have more control," Eve muttered knowing that her tormentor heard her plea.

As she was moved off the Stryker stretcher and onto the bed, the demon got in Eve's face as her restrained body was held on her side. Someone pulled the orange backboard out from under her. The staff laid her flat on the bed and ran white straps through both her wrists and ankles restraints, securing her firmly so she wouldn't fall off. The staff held Eve on her side as a nurse bent down, pulled her pants down off her hips, and injected medicine in her butt. As staff released the little psychic, a special wedge was slipped under the mattress so Eve could sit up.

The demon grabbed Eve by her chin and threatened, "*You don't give the orders in this arrangement. You have no power over me so stop thinking that you do or I will see to it that your time in here will be full of pain and suffering."*

All the staff left the side room, locking the door behind her. Muffled voices barely reached her ears as she replied to her tormentor, "Do whatever you want. It's not like I can stop you, but I'd like to know what's got you so frightened?"

"Nothing scares me, child! Don't project your own fear and claim it to mine. We both know you're not that bright, nor brave."

"What is the Reset supposed to mean?" The little psychic pressed, knowing full well that the demon would become more agitated. To Eve's surprise, her tormentor's face blanched so she added, "I know that you know what it means. Will you tell me about it?"

The demon growled as it grabbed the top of the little psychic's head, squeezing on it like a vise. Eve cried out in pain as she felt her tormentor reach inside her body, running its black claws across her organs. Eve retched in agony as a voice spoke to her from an intercom on the wall, "Eve, how can we help you?"

The little psychic bit out with her face scrunched up painfully, "Get this fucking demon off me!"

No response from the person in the ante room.

The demon ran its tongue over Eve's face, licking her tears, "*You want to know, do you? Here you go, Eve. Pain and suffering. That's what it represents. I'm just giving you a preview.*"

A pressure built up in Eve's head, one that wasn't related to the demon's attack. Eve clenched her jaw, grinding her teeth as the pain became unbearable. She opened her eyes, which glowed white, and bellowed loudly. Relief came as a pulse of psychic energy exploded violently from her head.

The blast caught the demon by surprise and rattled the two-way windows. He grunted painfully as his ethereal form was flung out of the side room. Eve leaned forward moaning, heavily heaving as her lips quivered. Her mouth gaped open as she searched the room for her tormentor.

The little psychic wondered what happened exactly. Her head felt light, but the throbbing pain from the demon remained. Eve ended up lying back down and passed out from exhaustion and the medicine.

Chapter Seven

"Ms. Driskell?" A voice spoke out, "Eve, are you awake?"

She woke up and glanced over to her left and saw a woman sticking her head out of a slightly ajar door. The little psychic nodded her sweat-glistened head, unsure how much time had passed. The woman walked in with several techs behind her. Eve blinked her eyes, trying to get the blurry vision to cease as the woman spoke, "I'm Dr Riggs. I'm here to assess you and see how you're doing this evening."

Mutely, Eve shrugged her shoulders. She didn't want to look at anyone. Dr Riggs stepped at the end of the bed, gazing at the top of the little psychic's head.

"Can you look up at me, Eve?" The doctor asked.

Eve looked at the doctor past several strands of her dirty blonde hair that was stuck to her clammy skin, her eyes were irritated and red.

"Hi there, Ms. Driskell. Can you tell me why you're in restraints?"

She shrugged her shoulders, "Because I'm a terrible person who should be punished."

"You're here because you attacked one of the staff. Do you know why you did it?"

Eve looked back down in shame, "The demon was hurting him so I tried to fight it off. I-I didn't want him to get hurt. Is he okay? How's his heart?"

"I'm not sure," Dr Riggs stated as she walked over to the side of the bed, "I'm here to check on you. To see if you feel like these are still necessary or not?"

Tears ran down the little psychic's cheek, splashing on her shirt, "I'm okay. I'm not a threat to anyone. I promise that I won't try to hurt myself or others."

The doctor speculatively eyed her, "I see. Is this demon in here with you now?"

Eve nervously looked all over the room. She wondered where her tormentor went to. Was it hiding in her room, waiting to pounce on her again? Why did it leave so abruptly? The little psychic locked her eyes with the doctor and shook her head, "I'm not sure where he's at. Let me out, please. I'll be good. I won't cause any more problems."

"Hmm, I'll see what I can do, Ms. Driskell," the doctor stated as she walked out the side door. She could hear the doctor talking with the staff. Mentally, Eve could feel their trepidation at the thought of releasing her.

She heard the main door to the side room unlock. It swung open and several techs stood by as the nurse ordered, "I'm going to let you out of these. Can you promise to behave? No more outbursts?"

"I just wanna go to my room. I won't even come out. Just let me out of these."

"Okay. Unlock them." The nurse stated and added, "If you get aggressive, these *will* go back on."

Eve meekly nodded as she looked down at her lap. Multiple hands groped at her wrists and ankles, unlocking the restraints. She could hear their thoughts as if they were speaking out loud. The woman next to her that was removing her right wrist was angry. She glared at the little psychic several times, blaming her for hurting Derek and several other people.

As the last of the restraints were taken off, Eve looked at the tech as she backed away. Tears streamed down her face as she spoke, "I'm sorry that I hurt your friend. I didn't mean to, but I don't blame you for being resentful. I guess that I would be too."

The nurse pointed at the door, "When you're ready, we will walk to your room."

Eve nodded as she slipped off the bed. She padded her way out of the side room with her head hung low, wondering where her shoes were at. The staff surrounded her, but gave Eve space just in case she chose to attack.

"Are you hungry? Would you like some juice or water?" One of the techs asked. Eve quickly shook her head as they went down the hallway. She was more concerned that her tormentor would be waiting for her in her room. The female tech walked ahead and unlocked Eve's room and pulled out the plastic chair.

She paused at the threshold and muttered, "I truly am sorry." Eve walked over to her bed and saw that someone had put her shoes next to it. The nurse spoke to Eve as curled up on the bed, "If you need anything, just let us know. Maggie will be just outside your door."

Eve looked over and saw Maggie. She sat down in the chair, still thinking about her friend Derek. She held the same folder that Derek had earlier and was adding to the doodle art, glancing up at the little psychic.

"I didn't mean to hurt him, Maggie. You've got to listen to me!"

The female tech looked up, feeling confused, "Did you say something, Eve?"

"I'm sorry that I attacked Derek."

"Don't worry about it." Maggie flatly stated, but Eve could hear her inner dialogue blaring out, loud and clear.

"Yeah right. It was the demon's fault. I'm innocent. Blah, blah, blah! Same shit story, different day. Crazy bitch! Why do I have to sit with her?"

"If you don't want to be here, you can ask someone else to relieve you, Maggie. I don't blame you for thinking that I'm a crazy bitch. Just know that the demon was hurting Derek and I had to stop it from damaging his heart."

Maggie's cheeks flushed for a moment, then she realized that she hadn't said anything. The tech watched Eve for a moment and then said, "I never called you that. I don't know where you got that from, but you should try and get some sleep."

Eve rolled over and clutched her thin blanket against her body with her eyes closed. She had the feeling that she was being watched and not just by Maggie. The little psychic wasn't sure if she wanted to acknowledge whatever entity it was. Eve knew that it wasn't her tormentor. The demon would've announced its presence with its usually derogatory statements.

Eve froze as she felt a hand caressing her cheek, wondering if whatever it was would try and molest her. An odd odor assailed her nose.

Jasmine.

She barely opened her eyes and saw a woman dressed in a tattered black robe. Her eyes pulsated and glowed purple. Eve wanted to move away, but the woman held her in place. It looked up at Maggie and smiled, "She can't see me nor hear my words, child. We need to talk, Eve, so use your inner voice with me. I will hear you."

"*What do you want from me?*" Eve mentally squeaked out.

"*Nothing, my child.*"

"*Then why are you here? Who are you?*"

The woman looked up at the ceiling for a moment, then answered, "*I used to have a name, but you will know me as the Protector. You need to be ready to leave this place.*"

Eve snorted. She glanced over her shoulder at Maggie. The tech didn't seem to notice her laugh or probably didn't care. The little psychic looked back at the woman and said, "*That's not happening any time soon. I'm stuck here and have no way out.*"

"*Ms. Driskell, I have someone coming here tonight that can help you leave here. Prepare, for when the time comes, you will need to be strong if you want to survive the Reset.*"

"*What is the Reset? I've heard others saying it, or at least it keeps getting repeated a lot in people's thoughts.*"

"*Your demon didn't say?*" The entity asked, yet Eve felt like she knew the answer.

"*He seemed frightened by it and then he took it out on me. I'm surprised that he's not here right now.*"

The woman chuckled, "*I'm not supposed to interfere or intervene, but I felt that you needed to hear me out, especially after you blasted him away from you while incapacitated.*"

"*You saw what happened? Please tell me how I made him go away. Or did you do it?*"

The female entity smiled proudly at the little psychic, "No, my child, that was all you. When you leave here, there will be much chaos and death. You'll need to hone your psychic abilities and join others like yourself if you're to survive the Reset."

"Is it the one on the horse that's coming in here?" Eve asked, hoping that it was so that she could finally meet this person.

"That one is here for you, but not the one who's coming here for you. I must go now, Eve. Heed the warning and prepare, for the Reset is coming."

Eve watched as the woman disappeared before her eyes. She wasn't sure what to make of this news. The little psychic pondered the fact that she actually attacked her tormentor and it affected him.

How can I do that again when I don't know what I did exactly?

Eve was tired and hurting, but sleep seemed to be eluding her. Her brain was hearing the thoughts of others along with her own racing thoughts. Eve wondered what she needed to do in order to be ready for the Reset. The Protector didn't exactly say what was going to happen, but Eve had a feeling that it was going to be terrible.

Chapter Eight

The morning sun came early as the little psychic stretched as she sat up on the side of the bed. She looked over at her tech as she padded over to the bathroom. Something seemed strange about him, his eyes appeared vacant as he stared at the folder in his lap.

"I'm going to the bathroom," Eve called out, expecting the tech to call another staff over so he could enter the room and observe her. Eve had grown accustomed to not having any privacy, especially since she was on watch.

"Go on. I don't care." The tech replied with a monotone voice.

Eve paused as the doorway, eyeing the man, "You're supposed to make sure that I don't hurt myself. Aren't you going to come in?"

The tech didn't reply. She shrugged her shoulders as she went into the bathroom. The little psychic kept getting a sickening feeling as she did her business. Hearing the thoughts of others around her, it seemed like it all centered on finding a way to exit.

Eve quickly wiped and flushed the toilet. As she walked over to the sink to wash her hands, she froze. The tech was standing behind her. She turned and looked at the man and saw that his eyes were clouded over and vacant. He smiled, but Eve knew that there was nothing humorous about what he was doing.

"Eve, do you know where I can find my exit?"

Perplexed, the little psychic asked, "I don't understand. What are you talking about?"

"My exit." The tech stated, "What are some things that I can use to exit here?"

Eve nervously shifted from foot to foot, "You work here so you have a badge and a set of keys that unlocks the doors. Why don't you use those?"

The tech smiled blissfully as he reached into his pants pocket and pulled out his keys. He placed several keys in between his fingers and stated, "Why didn't I think of this. Thanks, Eve, for helping me with my exit."

To Eve's horror, the tech repeatedly punched himself in the neck with his keys. He managed to puncture his carotid artery; blood gushed out like a ship that crashed into a cluster of rocks. He dropped down to the floor, smiling.

Eve quickly turned and dropped to her knees, clutching the sides of her toilet. She puked all the contents of her stomach, which was mostly bile. She wiped her mouth with the back of her hand before crying out, "Staff! I need help in here!"

No immediate response.

"Staff!" Eve frantically screamed as she stood up. She carefully stepped over the dead body, barely missing his blood that colored the floor. The little psychic had an uneasy feeling as she slipped her rubber shoes on and walked towards the door.

Her eyes widened as she saw ghosts that were no longer shadowy figures, each one had more definition and appeared to be more solid. People were wandering the unit like zombies, shambling about with the same vacant gaze as her tech had before he killed himself.

Several of the other patients were banging their heads on the metal window frame on the wall. A staff member was pushing something metallic in an electrical outlet. Eve was bombarded by frenzied thoughts, ones filled with hate and lust. The little psychic ran down the hallway, looking for a way to escape the unit.

She abruptly stopped at The Bubble and saw several staff attacking each other. The victims weren't fighting back, just blissfully smiling as they were punched and repeatedly stabbed with pens. One woman was pinned to the door, her clothes had been torn off and two guys took turns molesting her.

Eve ran over and snatched a badge and a set of keys from a tech that had died from a pair of scissors in her heart. Tears streamed down Eve's face as she fled to the double doors exit. As she swiped the badge over the electronic reader, the little psychic heard multiple footfalls behind her. She turned and saw several nurses and a few female patients glaring at her, their eyes were completely black and they had foamy brown spittle dripping from their mouths.

"It's time for some fun," one patient coldly uttered, "Come here so we can *all* have fun playing with you, Eve."

Eve pushed on the main exit doors, but they didn't budge. Frantically, she swiped the badge over the reader and rushed out the double doors. Eve scurried down the short corridor. She swiped the badge again to unlock the door that led to the stairwell.

The little psychic sprinted down the stairs, feeling a panic attack coming on as she heard the stairwell door open and slam shut. Snarls and grunts echoed throughout the stairwell. Their dark thoughts echoed loudly in Eve's mind as she reached the ground floor.

Eve scanned the badge over the electronic reader and searched for something, anything, that she could wedge the door shut, but there was nothing. Eve groaned as she fled down the winding corridors, every section required the use of an electronic reader to open the heavy metal doors. Each section had dead bodies strewn on the floor.

As she exited from the building, Eve wasn't sure which way to go, let alone leave the hospital. She ran down the long walkway, hoping to see a hint of light in this dark hell she was experiencing. Eve looked to her right and saw more dead bodies. Some from suicide and others at the hands of deranged people. Eyes glared at the little psychic from the plaza.

The crazed people ran towards her, each person had bloody torn clothes. Eve glanced over her shoulder and saw her pursuers from her ward poured out of the building. The little psychic knew that if any of them caught her that her life would be forfeit, but not before they hurt her.

The plethora of voices became so overwhelming that Eve clutched her head, crying. The little psychic was too distraught that she didn't notice a dark figure in front of her. She collided with it, knocking her down on the concrete walkway. Eve looked up and, to her horror, stood a demon.

Her personal tormentor.

He looked down at the little psychic, tsking as he shook his head. The demon always took pleasure in knocking her on her ass, "I see that you've made more friends since we last spoke. Why do you run when you know that you deserve their gifts of pain and suffering?"

Eve scrambled backwards but collapsed, the sensory overload more painful. She curled up in a fetal position, screaming. She barely registered the marching cadence of many footfalls, but felt many hands grabbing at her. Eve was forcefully yanked up to her feet and slammed hard against the brick wall.

The demon was about to mock Eve more, but was tackled to the ground as more crazed people filled the area. He seemed genuinely surprised and confused at the same time.

"How is this possible? I'm not of this world! You can't physically touch me!"

Several Ferals leaned down and gnawed on his thick leathery flesh. He groaned, baring his razor-sharp teeth as a crazed man leaned down and stated, "Welcome to *our* world, you ugly fuck! You're different and tougher than the ones we've played with here. More fun for us. Finding other ways to make you suffer. You're a part of this world now and we're here to greet you properly."

"Impossible!" The demon blurted out. He managed to see his favorite *student* and glared, "You did this to me, Eve! You and your magic! How did you manage making me physically here?"

Eve couldn't reply, let alone think, as her small body was assailed by multiple fists. A Feral woman licked Eve's face then she banged the little psychic's head forcefully against the brick wall.

"Come on. Let me eat your lovely brain!" The Feral woman hissed.

Eve didn't know what to do and death seemed like the best option, but a familiar female voice spoke to her, drowning out all the other voices, "*That's not your fate today, Eve. Your way out is here to help so don't freak out when you see him.*"

Eve groaned as hands groped her body, but the pressure from her attackers lessened. Screams and painful grunts filled the air. Dazed from the head trauma, Eve barely made out the word exchange from the Feral woman and her rescuer.

"You can't have this one, *monster*! Her deranged brain is mine to harvest!"

"Have you looked in a mirror lately? That will show you who the real *monster* is."

The woman snarled as she lunged, leaving Eve to drop in a heap. She cringed at the sound of cracking bones. Eve flinched at a pair of hands grabbing her and she smelled the scent of strawberry. Several Ferals turned and rushed towards the interloper. Eve's tormentor growled as he teleported himself away from the Ferals. He pointed a clawed finger as he roared, "Hands off what is rightfully mine! You have no claim to her."

Whomever held Eve didn't reply as he teleported away.

Chapter Nine

Eve fell down onto her hands and knees, emptying the miniscule contents of her stomach. The little psychic heaved more than what came out, her muscles spasmed painfully. Eve collapsed on her side, feeling the effects of her head trauma and unable to move right.

"Where...am I?" Eve groaned out.

"Not far from where you were imprisoned," a deep masculine voice answered soothingly, "We're still not safe. Can you walk?"

"Are you... asking me...to dance?" Eve asked as she had a laughing fit.

"That answers that question," the entity stated with a wry smile. He looked around, searching for his partner. "Where the hell are you, Fal?"

"What's a Fal?" Eve asked as she unsteadily sat up. She blinked several times, trying to focus on the man that had rescued her. Her head hurt from both the physical and psychic beating.

"Fal is my raid partner and it appears that he's been delayed elsewhere."

The little psychic froze as she saw him, her mouth gaped open in fear. The creature before her had crimson and brown skin that seemed dry like leather and had slick black hair. His eyes had the characteristics of a goat. It wore gray cargo pants that hung low on its hips. A tattered, sleeveless biker vest and black leather boots completed his ensemble.

She slowly scrambled backwards, crying out, "No, no, no! It can't be! Not another demon!"

The demon's lips parted slightly, feeling confused, he stated, "Of course I'm a demon. Didn't you notice earlier?"

"Go away!" Eve screeched as she picked up and threw handfuls of rocks at the demon, "Why must you torture me?"

The demon dodged the volley by teleporting out of the way. Eve fell back on to her back, hysterically cackling, "Why not? This is my life! Of course, a fucking demon saves me!"

The demon stood next to the little psychic, puzzled by her. He reached down and pulled Eve up to him. She lost her hysterical antics and meekly muttered, "Don't hurt me."

"Ms. Driskell," the demon replied as he gazed at her with his goat-slit eyes, "I'm not here to hurt you. I was sent to save you."

"Lies!" Eve bit out as she tried to escape his grasp, "There's no such thing as a good demon, they don't exist."

The demon pouted, "You wound me with your harsh words, Eve. My type is few and rare. My name is Moneek, by the way."

Eve paused. She narrowed her eyes suspiciously at the demon, "Did...did you just give me your true name or fake one?"

"It's my true name and I give it to you freely, in the name of trust."

Eve glared at the demon, still unwilling to trust him. She trusted one once and ended up with her own personal tormentor. Malicious snarls broke the tension as a horde of Ferals scampered down the street towards them. Moneek pushed the little psychic behind him protectively, growling at the incoming threat.

"I hear that you're a psychic. What kind of abilities do you have at your disposal, Eve? Eve?"

He glanced behind him and saw the little psychic crouched down on the ground, clutching her head. "Too. Many. Thoughts. Can't. Stop. Them!"

Moneek grunted, knowing that he was Eve's only line of defense. His hands clenched tightly, glowing with a sickly green energy. The demon let loose his magical energy, Ferals screamed in agony when struck by it.

"Block it, Eve!" Moneek ordered, but at the same time, he wondered where his partner was at. "Shield your mind!"

Eve cried out, "Can't!"

Sweat beaded on the demon's face from his magical exertion. No matter how many Ferals he took down, more seemed to replace them at an astonishing rate. As the crazed people encroached on them, the sound of heavy hooves thundered behind the Ferals.

Moneek was relieved to see his partner barreling through the horde on his war horse, slashing his swords effortlessly at any that neared him. The demon noticed that Fal'destion wasn't alone. Someone was riding behind him, casting magical energy and using it as a barrier.

The barrier not only stopped any attackers, it knocked them back like their bodies were struck by lightning. Moneek was impressed by this person's magical talent.

Fal slowed his steed next to the demon and spoke, his voice was both melodious and monotone, "What's wrong with the girl?"

"Sensory overload and a terrible beating," the demon answered.

"Why haven't you gotten her back to the facility already," Fal grumbled.

"You have to take her back. She's got a concussion and I'm not risking her life by teleporting us that long of a distance. She could die."

The other rider with Fal slipped off the war horse and walked over to Eve. The woman had red hair and dressed similar to Eve. She looked up at the men and stated, "I'll hold off the freaks and buy you time to get my girl out of here. Got it, elf?"

Fal sneered slightly, as he dismounted, "I'm a *Fae* warrior, not an Elf. Big difference, Jayne."

Moneek kept up his magical attacks as Red Jayne placed her hands on the ground. A magical bubble of pure energy encased them, creating a protective shield. Fal and the demon managed to lift Eve up and draped her onto the war horse's back sideways. The fae warrior straddled his body next to the little psychic as Moneek held her in place.

"So, what's the plan?" Moneek asked.

"We ride north, back to the facility. You two take one of those vehicles." He pointed at a nearby parking lot. The fae warrior looked down at the energy worker and said, "Jayne said that she has the mental prowess to get one working without a key."

"Commandeering is my specialty," Red Jayne quipped.

The demon nodded as he looked at the redheaded woman. She was straining to keep the shield in place as more Ferals battered at it.

"Once you let go of your protection, I'll teleport us to the parking lot."

Fal unsheathed his two swords and, with a quick command in his native tongue, urged his steed into a full gallop. Moneek looked at the woman and commented, "I guess that's your cue, energy master. Let them have it."

Red Jayne grinned; her hair danced in the air as she let her protective shield go. It mowed down any in its path, like the shockwave from an explosive device. Bodies flew in the air, their limbs flailing as the fae warrior rushed by.

Eve closed her eyes, trying to calm her mind and not overstimulate it by watching the ground swiftly and the clacking of thundering hooves. Fal'destion swiftly slashed at any Feral that came near them with little effort. The voices seemed to lessen the further they rode, but the little psychic's head pounded.

She heard the rider say something unintelligible, which caused the war horse to come to a halt. Eve blinked as she looked up at the rider. What did Moneek call him, a fae warrior? He had pale, perfect skin with long flowing blonde hair and pointy ears. His clothes were colorful, bright yellow, green, and blue. His leggings, as well as the tunic he wore, was form fitting and he had calf high leather boots.

"Where are you taking me?"

Fal glanced down at the little psychic and said calmly, "Somewhere safe, little one."

Eve grimaced, "Do you have anything for a headache? My head is throbbing."

"I rarely carry medicinal herbs with me. That's what healers are for. I'm no healer, child." The fae warrior stated coldly as he dismounted.

"Who are you and why have you been following me?" Eve asked as he assisted her to the ground, noticing that they were on the bank of a river. She clutched her head as she buried her face in his chest. The fae warrior ushered her to sit under a nearby tree. The little psychic pressed her head against her knees, rocking slightly as she grasped the sides of her head. He walked over to his war horse and led it to the river's edge. Fal took a piece of cloth from a satchel and wet it in the running waters.

Eve felt something wet on the back of her neck so she glanced up at the fae warrior squatting in front of her. She closed her eyes and meekly muttered, "Thank you."

"My name is Fal'destion and I'm a fae warrior. I've been keeping a close watch on you for a while now."

"Why would you? Why didn't you approach me until today?"

"It wasn't time for introductions. Moneek and I have been scouting around for some time, trying to find those that have gifts."

"But," Eve squeaked out, "why didn't you try talking to me before now?"

Fal stood up and stated, "I couldn't speak to you because you were in places that had high concentrations of iron. It's lethal to my kind. I can be near it, but it weakens me. I didn't want to speak to you mentally because I knew that you were having a difficult time during this transitional period of your world."

The little psychic wasn't sure what to make of all this. She felt that strange pressure building up in her head, like when she was in the side room. The fae warrior backed away, grabbing his steed by the reins and moving it behind a large boulder. Eve cried out painfully, "What's wrong with me? What's happening?"

At that moment, her tormentor appeared in front of her. The demon tsked at the little psychic, "Poor pathetic Eve. I can't leave you alone for five minutes without you wandering off. I suppose it's fitting, you never were that smart."

"Leave me alone," Eve bit out as she cried.

"Don't think so, stupid girl. You will never be alone and I'm going to punish you for trying to hurt me."

"I think it's time for you to leave, demon," Fal muttered as he held up the edge of a dagger against the demon's throat, surprising it.

"This doesn't concern you," the demon coldly replied, "This one is bound to me. I'm her teacher and-"

"You're nothing but an abusive cretin. I should end you right now, demon." Fal said calmly, which made Eve look up. She wondered if the fae warrior was capable of expressing any emotions. Fal added, "I should let her take you out with one of her psychic blasts. It was amusing seeing her do it to you the last time."

The demon snarled, "You know nothing of what happened in that room. I left of my own accord. I'll show you!"

The demon threw an elbow in Fal'destion's ribs, causing him to grunt. Eve's tormentor teleported himself away from the fae warrior and appeared next to the little psychic. He grabbed her and roughly yanked Eve to her feet. The demon extended his black claws and wrapped his fingers around her throat.

Fal stepped forward, but stopped as the demon threatened, "Take another step and I will rip her throat out and bathe in her blood! I beg you to do it."

Fal eyed the demon and then looked into Eve's eyes and mentally spoke to her, "*I see your power building in your head, child. Use it on him if you wish to live.*"

Tears streamed down her face, her eyes pleading with the fae warrior, "*But I don't know how to do that. I don't even know how I did it the first time.*"

"Disarm, Fae!" The demon ordered as he dug his claws into Eve's flesh, drawing blood. "I won't ask again."

Fal let his dagger drop to the ground, never taking his eyes off the little psychic. "*Push it out. It's going to be painful on me, but it beats the alternative, Eve. Scream and let all your pain and humiliation that he's put you through and give it a voice!"*

"*All* of them. I'm not playing around. I will kill her. I can find a better toy to play with."

"*I don't know...I don't want to hurt you. It seems like that's all I do lately. I hurt all those that try to help me.*"

Fal methodically reached for his swords. "*Do it now, child. I will survive, just do it. Fuel it with your anger and frustration.*"

The little psychic screamed loudly, causing the demon to grip her throat tighter, "Silence, you pathetic girl! You-"

Eve croaked out as her eyes glowed white, "Leave me alone!"

A strong blast of psychic energy exploded from her head. The blast threw her tormentor up in the air, toppling over into the river. The fae warrior was thrown against the boulder, where he crumpled in a heap. Eve dropped to her knees. She watched as the river swept her tormentor away. She wasn't sure if the demon was dead or merely unconscious, but Eve hoped that she would be long gone from here.

She looked over at the downed fae warrior. Eve wasn't sure if she killed him or not. Her thoughts went dark as she looked down at the ground.

"No matter what I do. I end up hurting everyone around me. Why did he make me hurt him?"

The squealing of brakes brought the little psychic out of her thoughts. She glanced over and saw a silver Chevy pickup come to a stop. Jayne and Moneek stepped out and rushed over. She kneeled down by the fae warrior and examined him. Moneek approached Eve with his hands up to show that he wasn't a threat.

"What did you do to him, Eve?" Red Jayne growled, causing her to flinch. "I know it was you because I sensed your power as we got closer. He's here to help you, damn it!"

"I hurt everyone. You know this. Might as well leave me here."

The demon paused as he saw the little psychic's neck. He got the heavy scent of sulphur, "Your demon was here, wasn't he?"

Eve shrugged her shoulders meekly while rubbing her arm as she muttered, "What does it matter? I'm not worth saving."

"Where's your fucking demon? I don't see him!" Jayne demanded as she stormed over to Eve. The energy worker towered over the little psychic with her fists clenched. "You need to take some responsibility for your actions for once in your life!"

Moneek stepped protectively in front of Eve, "We need to get back to the facility, not standing here fighting each other."

"You don't scare me, demon! Why I ought to-"

"Shut up and listen to my friend," Fal said, interrupting Jayne's tirade. Eve dared to look up and around the demon at the fae warrior. She nervously nibbled on her bottom lip as he spoke calmly. "She did what she had to in order to survive. I told her to do it so leave her alone."

"You don't understand, Fal," Red Jayne pointed an accusatory finger at Eve, "She doesn't understand that her actions have consequences. I don't-"

Fal put a hand up, silencing her, "Moneek is right. We need to get back to the facility. Come, ride with me Jayne."

Jayne looked at Eve and then back at Fal, "I don't know. She's in no shape to drive. I wouldn't trust her to do that simple task."

"I can drive," Moneek announced with a smile, "I watched how she did it, despite having to white knuckle it all the way here. How hard can it be?"

Jayne glared at the demon, but walked over to the fae warrior. Fal looked at the demon for a moment and then muttered a word in his native language. His war horse trotted forward, snorting and ready to go. The fae warrior climbed up on the horse's back, barely grunting in pain, and extended his hand to Jayne.

Eve stood up and had a panicked look on her face, "You two are going to leave me? With this demon?"

Jayne humorlessly snorted as she mounted herself in front of Fal. She nestled her back against him and stated, "That's rich coming from someone that made a deal with one. Get me to this place you two keep going on about."

Fal spurred the war horse forward and admonished calmly, "You need to learn tact. Eve has her own problems, as do you. She needs actual guidance, not berating from a friend."

She glared at Eve, who looked away in shame, "I'll try, but-"

"No buts, Jayne. Tough love comes later. Now, we need to get you both to safety so you both can get a better grasp on this world's current situation."

As they trotted away, Moneek turned around and looked at the little psychic. Eve's lips quivered as she looked up at the demon. She wasn't sure what to think of him. This demon hasn't hurt her, yet. He reached out for her hand and Eve instinctively flinched.

"I'm not going to hurt you, Eve. I never will, but we need to get you out of here before any Ferals finds us. Or your other demonic *friend*."

Eve ran towards the truck. She hopped in the passenger side and locked her door. Moneek walked over, cautiously surveying his surroundings. He placed his hand on the hood of the truck and muttered an incantation in both Latin and his demonic tongue.

Eve felt uncomfortable as the magic filled the cab of the truck. The demon opened the driver's side door and slipped behind the wheel. He looked at the little psychic as he scratched his head.

"So, the R means run and the D means dash, right?" the demon cackled as Eve's eyes widened.

She smacked his arm, "That's not funny. Do you know how to drive or not?"

Moneek glanced at the little psychic playfully, "You're about to find out, Eve."

Chapter Ten

Eve kept her eyes closed as the demon darted across the lanes of the highway without a care in the world. He rolled down his window and stuck his head out, letting his tongue dangle out like a dog.

"This is so much fun! I told you that I can drive." The demon shouted.

Eve gulped, "That's debatable."

"Oh, come on," Moneek pouted, "I haven't hit anything in the last two miles."

She looked at the demon, "The point of driving is to get from point A to point B without having an accident."

"But what's the fun in that?" The demon asked as he moved his head back into the cab.

Eve shook her head, "You're making me nervous and I don't want to do something that could kill us both." She slumped her shoulders, "I deserve to die."

Moneek looked at Eve and said, "No, you don't. You deserve to live. Don't let anyone tell you otherwise, not even yourself, Eve."

"Why do you even care what happens to me? I'm nothing special. I'm just a demon's punching bag. You might as well get your shots in too."

"You're the mind reader, you tell me."

The little psychic refused to listen to the demon's thoughts. She was barely keeping her mind focused so that she could stop the thoughts from the clusters of Ferals that fought to be heard. Eve leaned forward with her head in her hands. She felt a hand on her thigh and heard Moneek say, "Keep it together, Eve. We're almost there."

"I-I don't know if I can," the little psychic glanced over at the demon, her eyes showed fear, "My head is...getting worse... please kill me..."

"Out of the question! Block it out, Eve!" Moneek replied with panic lacing his voice. He pressed down on the gas pedal, swerving past the many parked vehicles along the highway. He looked out the window and saw Fal and Red Jayne riding next to them.

The demon met the fae warrior's eyes and pointed at Eve. He nodded and urged his steed forward; the war horse was able to run faster than the truck because of its magical connection. The demon watched as the riders plowed a path through a crowd of Ferals, he hoped that it would help Eve, but it didn't.

She groaned in pain as she curled up on her side, her head resting on Moneek's thigh. He gently put a clawed hand on her shoulder, "Hang in there, kid. Just another few minutes."

Several thumps from the back of the truck bed caught the demon's attention. He looked over his shoulder and saw several Ferals had managed to crawl in the back of the speeding truck. The crazed men were covered in blood and had gashes on their torsos and faces, their clothes in tatters.

They crawled towards the cab, banging on the back glass. Moneek glared as he bared his teeth at the Ferals. Eve moaned, "Make it stop! Make it stop!"

"Stop?" One Feral rasped, "We haven't begun to defile either of you. Stop the truck and let us play with you both."

"I want to devour your entrails, little girl. Maybe gorge myself on your heart," another man hissed as he smacked at the glass, "Feed my hunger, bitch!"

Moneek yanked on the steering wheel, careening the truck into a spin as he slammed on the brake pedal. The Ferals collided with each other before toppling out of the truck bed. The demon put the truck in park, locked the doors, and stated, "Stay put, Eve. I'm going to deal with them."

Eve looked at Moneek through bleary eyes. She saw him wink with a malicious grin before vanishing before her eyes. She heard muffled grunts and screaming coming from outside. The truck bucked back and forth at times as bodies crashed into it. She felt the pressure building up in her brain once more.

What's wrong with me?

Something heavy crashed onto the roof of the cab. Eve frantically searched for the cause and saw her tormentor gazing back at her through the windshield. He ran his claws along the glass. He appeared angry and frustrated as he spoke, "Eve. Open the door and let me take you away from all of this. I promise to be nice to you."

The little psychic rolled over, clutching her head, and buried her face in the soft bench seat. The demon roared as he slammed his fists at the glass, but the windshield didn't break.

"Open the door and let me in, you stupid girl!"

Moneek reappeared inside the cab, sitting behind the wheel. He grinned at Eve's tormentor as he mocked, "Aww, what's the matter? Can't get in here to collect your prize? It sucks being a negative ass like you. I got in just fine. Someone is having an off day today."

The demon pointed at Moneek, growling angrily, "You're a disgrace to all of demon kind! Give her to me now and I shall let you live."

Moneek chuckled, "Come inside here and get her yourself. Oh wait, you can't. The warding on this vehicle is in place, just for you. That said," he put the truck into gear, pressing the gas pedal down, "let's go for a little ride!"

The back tires squealed as the truck lurched forward down the highway. Eve's tormentor had a difficult time holding on. He growled out before teleporting away, "I will get you; you hear me! You can't hide from me, Eve Driskell! I *will* find you!"

They drove for a few more miles in complete silence, except for Eve crying out in pain. Moneek slammed on the brakes when the old military facility came into view. The truck slowed down as it entered an open garage door, where Fal'destion and Red Jayne waited patiently for them. The demon put the truck in park and opened the door. He reached for Eve, but she released a pulse of psychic energy.

Moneek grunted as he was thrown into the concrete wall. Eve sat up with her eyes glowing, her face was scrunched in pain as she climbed out of the cab. Red Jayne ran over to grab the little psychic, but she got knocked back by another psychic pulse from her. Fal leaned down and protected the energy worker as Eve walked outside of the facility.

She clenched her hands as more waves of psychic energy exploded from her. She wasn't sure what was happening to her and no idea how to stop it. The little psychic dropped down to her knees as more psychic pulses spilled out of her.

She flinched when a pair of hands grabbed her shoulders. She cried out, "Get back! I can't stop it!"

She heard an unknown female's voice speak to her, "You're safe now. Go to sleep."

Eve felt her entire body respond as it relaxed. As she closed her eyes and fell forward, the same woman caught her and the little psychic caught a whiff of cinnamon before blacking out.

Chapter Eleven

Eve woke up in what appeared to be a hospital bed. *Fitting,* she thought. She tried to sit up, but was greeted with the sound of metal clanking against the rails of the bed. She looked down and saw that her hands were held in place by strange looking restraints. They had strange markings etched into the metal and they seemed to glow at times.

Great. Back in restraints again. It must be my lot in life to end up in them.

Eve felt tears welling up in her eyes as she slumped her head and shoulders in shame. The little psychic shook her head slowly, wondering what's the point of living if this was going to be her reality.

Did I trade one prison for another?

Eve was so wrapped up in her despair that she barely felt a hand on her shoulder. The little psychic cried out, "I'm not a danger to myself or anyone else! Please, I don't want to be in here like this!"

Eve's body jerked as she took in quick breaths, feeling all alone with just her thoughts. *At least the voices have stopped,* Eve thought and then she caught the scent of cinnamon coming from her right. She bit her trembling bottom lip as she nervously turned her head.

"Hi, Eve. How are you doing today? Are you feeling better?" The strange woman asked. She had long silky black hair and wore black form fitting clothes. Eve shrugged her shoulders as she cast her eyes down, but didn't say a word.

"My name is Meg. I'm the reason that you're in these lovely devices. Are you hungry? I brought a sandwich and a bottle of wine."

The little psychic gave Meg a sideways look, "That's not proper protocol for a mental facility."

"Good thing we aren't in one of those places," Meg grinned as she gently brushed back Eve's hair from her petite face. "What's the last thing you remember before waking up here?"

Eve gasped, "Pain. Unbearable pain in my head. I couldn't stop it. I've hurt people, I know I did. It's what happens to anyone who tries being helpful to me. I suppose it was inevitable that I'd wake up like this. You should leave before I hurt you too."

Meg chuckled, "I'm not worried about that, Eve. Your powers are being neutered by these cuffs. I heard that you can hear other people's thoughts. Can you hear mine?"

The little psychic listened intently as she stared at the woman by her bedside. Tears streamed down her face as she emotionally croaked out, "No, I can't. What did you do to me?"

"Nothing." Meg replied as she lowered the bed rail. She sat down next to Eve on the bed. "I was taught to put up a mental barrier so that you wouldn't be overwhelmed by my emotional baggage. Trust me when I say, I have plenty of it to spare. It may also be the cuffs doing it, but-"

Eve's eyes brighten with a glimmer of hope, "Can I keep these on? I won't cause any trouble. I promise to be a good patient, doctor."

Meg leaned forward and pulled Eve into a loving embrace, "I'm not a doctor, but I'm a witch so close enough I guess."

The little psychic felt confused. She meekly muttered, "But I don't understand. You said that you were responsible for me being in these restraints. If you're not a doctor, then what did you mean?"

Meg leaned back and stated, "I was the only one who could get close enough to you to stop you. My magical shielding absorbed the brunt of your psychic assaults. I have the ability to make my magic do whatever I command it to do so I put you to sleep."

"It was you?" Eve opened her mouth slightly, "You put me to sleep and stopped me?"

Meg nodded. Eve smiled and said, "Thank you. I don't know what would've happened if you hadn't done what you did. Where have you been all of my life? Why couldn't you have worked at the hospitals where I was forced to stay?"

"I lived in Portland, doing freelance graphic designing." The witch sheepishly smirked, "I'm not a people person. I kept to myself and that career helped me avoid people easy enough. Now I'm going to try something."

The little psychic wearily eyed the witch as she stood up, "What're you going to do?"

"I'm going to drop my mental barrier. I want to test if the cuffs actually do stop your mind reading ability."

Eve panicked, "No! Don't! I want to be like this. It's so peaceful and I'm...scared!"

Meg parted her lips as she lowered her mental barrier, feeling guilty, but she had no choice. Adoy wanted this information about the little psychic so he could have a better understanding of what he had to work with. Meg watched as Eve softly cried, "Don't make me do it. I beg you."

"It's not my call, little miss know-it-all," the witch replied sympathetically, "Our magical teacher wanted me for this because..."

As she hesitated, Eve heard her thoughts and could literally feel every horrible emotion that ran rampant in her mind. The little psychic parted her lips, "You were recently hurt badly, both physically and emotionally. You're afraid of not being good enough for anyone or anything, even in this place. Terror. Trauma. Sexual abuse. Oh no!"

"What's wrong?"

Eve grimaced as she instinctively reached to clutch her head, but the restraints kept her from doing it. The little psychic painfully bit out, "Too. Much. To. Bare. No more! Make. It. Stop."

"I'm so sorry!" Meg babbled as she hastily put her mental barrier back in place. She sat down on the bed again and hugged Eve, stroking her back soothingly, "Everyone here is learning to guard their thoughts and not just because of you so don't think that's the reason. It's a skill that we all will need for what's coming."

"Oh." Eve muttered, but smiled as she added, "Are you sure that you're not psychic too?"

"Far from it, little miss know-it-all. I was informed that you tend to internalize many things. I know all about that because I do the same thing. Adoy wanted me to do this test because I've got enough emotional baggage that can easily overfill the Grand Canyon." She pulled back and pressed her forehead against Eve's forehead and proclaimed, "I swear to you that I will do my damnedest to keep my thoughts shut down for your sake."

Tears escaped from Eve's eyes, "Why are you being so nice to me? More than likely I will hurt you. Why bother?"

"Because you're in need of a friend and I'm willing to quell my moody side, just a little bit, so you don't needlessly suffer. I don't want to hurt you, Eve." Meg chuckled as she added, "I'd say read my mind, but I'm blocking you now."

Eve sighed as she smiled, "I can't hear you, but I can feel that you are being sincere somehow. I don't know what to think any more. Is Adoy the magical teacher?"

The witch snorted as she answered, "Yes and, between you and me, he reminds me of Yoda."

Eve nodded, but felt confused, so Meg patted her head and said with a confident smile as she stood up, "When you see him, I'm sure it will be clear."

The door to the room opened and in stepped Adoy. He was probably two and a half feet tall and had wrinkly green skin and no hair anywhere. His hands and feet had four digits with marble white claws at the ends. The rest of his body was covered with a gray, skin-tight bodysuit. Eve let out a slight giggle, getting the witch's Star Wars reference.

"Hello, Ms. Driskell. I'm Adoy. I'm the one that will be teaching you how to control your gifts and properly use them."

The little psychic glanced at the witch mischievously, "At least he talks normally and not all backwards."

"What do you mean by that?" The magical teacher asked. He eyed Meg and saw she was smirking, "I imagine that you told her something about me that you think is so amusing for whatever reason?"

"Me?" The witch grinned brightly, "I have nothing to do with it. You know that I'm a respectful witch."

Adoy raised his brow slightly, "You have the manners of a goat. Knowing you, you reversed my name and called me a Jedi Master. Whatever that is. You can go now, Meg. I can take it from here."

Meg turned and hugged the little psychic again and giggled, "Go, I must. Good relation with the Wookiees I have. Take care, Eve. Soon, I will see you."

Adoy shook his head as he put a tiny hand on his forehead, "Out, witch! Take your snark with you and stop filling her head with such nonsense."

Meg bowed dramatically as she replied before leaving, "As you command, my master!"

The magical teacher shook his head and then focused on the little psychic. He disappeared and reappeared on the bed where he sat down and asked, "What do you know about what's happening to you?"

Eve looked away in shame as she shrugged her shoulders, "I'm completely out of control. I'm hurting people whether I want to or not, unlike before."

"How so, child?"

"Do you really want to know?"

Adoy nodded curtly, "I do. It helps me to know what you need to learn and what you know. Tell me so I can help you get out of these restraints."

"I'm not sure if there's anything anyone can do for me."

"Good."

The little psychic looked at the little creature, feeling confused, "Huh? How's that a good thing?"

"It means that you know that no one can fix your condition. This is because no one understands what you are and how to help. I can guide you, but you have to take responsibility and put in a lot of hard work and training."

She kept darting her eyes from him and her lap, fidgeting with the blanket near her hands, "I can try, but if I can't do this will you kill me?"

"Do you believe that I'm anything like your demon?" Adoy asked.

"No. Not yet, but that can easily change."

"For your sake, as well as everyone else here at our facility, I will be harsh and firm with you. I'm not cruel, but I expect you to listen to what I have to offer because if we can't rein in your psychic talents, you *will* be put out of your misery. Does that sound fair, Eve?"

Eve nodded, "It's what I'd prefer to happen. I feel like I'm just going to disappoint everyone here and hurt a lot of innocent people in the process."

"Was you able to read Meg's thoughts?"

"Only when she let me. It was terrible. How does she carry on?"

Adoy eyed her intently, "You know the answer to that already. How do you carry on with what you've had to endure to this point?"

Eve thought for a moment and then said reluctantly, "Not well. I tried to kill myself, even before my brain went crazy." She bitterly laughed, "I'm a crazy girl. I wouldn't get too invested in me. I'll only disappoint you, Yoda."

"It's Adoy. Damn that witch. She has others reversing my name here like a damn palindrome." The little creature said with frustration.

"Sorry," Eve hung her head in shame, "it won't happen again."

"I blame Meg, not you. She's been helping me teach others here and insists on telling people *that's* my actual name. That said, read my thoughts."

Eve bit her bottom lip nervously, but Adoy stated, "Don't fret, child. I have more control over my thoughts and emotions than the witch. So, proceed so I can learn more

150

about your gifts and where you are lacking and which parts are strong."

Eve did as Adoy asked. She opened up her senses and peered into his mind. The little psychic listened intently and heard nothing. She looked at the magical teacher and asked, "I'm not sure if it's working or not."

"You're doing well, child," Adoy answered mentally, causing the little psychic to gasp, *"As you can tell, my mind is open, but it's not as chaotic as to what you're used to hearing, is it?"*

Eve wanted to see if she could talk to him mentally. It was always a one-sided conversation, even her tormentor didn't let it occur. She gulped as she spoke mentally, *"Can you hear me?"*

"Of course, I can, Eve. In this state of mind, you can speak to anyone you wish. Have you never tried it?"

She looked away, feeling like a fool, *"No. I didn't know that it was possible. I was taught how to invade other people's minds, but never thought actual communication was possible. My demon could speak to me like this, but I always spoke out loud. I've never had proper guidance. Will you be my guide?"*

"*First things first, Eve,*" Adoy replied as he pulled out a small piece of jewelry from his pocket. She watched as he poured magic into it and listened to his mental incantation, though she didn't understand it.

He looked at the little psychic and said out loud, "I'm going to give you this." The charm dangled from a gold chain in his tiny fingers. "It will work similar to these restraints, but not as strong so you will be able to use and harness your psychic abilities. I say this because you need to practice and hone your skills because you will need them in the war that's brewing on the horizon. Do you understand?"

Eve nodded. She wasn't sure what to think about the war he spoke about. Eve wasn't good at fighting; despite the many assaults and altercations she's been in during her short life. If she couldn't fight off her tormentor, then what good would she be in a real battle.

"You're selling yourself short, Eve." Adoy admonished, causing the little psychic to wonder if she spoke or if he heard her thoughts. "You've successfully fought off your demonic tormentor twice since the Reset began with no psychic training. I know others got caught in the wake of your wild magic, but if you let me teach you, just imagine what you could accomplish. That demon won't stand a chance against you, of this I'm sure. Now, lean forward and let me place this around your neck."

Eve leaned forward the best that she could. Adoy slipped the necklace over her head and let it drop against her chest, just at the cleavage line. It felt cold at first, but it eventually became warm. The little psychic watched the magical creature wave his hand and instantly the restraints were unlocked.

Eve was wary of taking her hands out of the magical devices. It felt good to be calm and centered for the first time in a long time. Adoy slipped off the bed and lowered one of the bed rails. He looked at the bedside table and saw a sandwich sitting next to a glass of wine. Adoy shook his head, "I guess Meg likes you well enough to share her wine with you. I'm surprised that it's still there."

Eve giggled as she looked at the meal that the witch left. She didn't know Meg at all and yet, she left her food and alcohol. *Maybe we can be friends.*

"You're free, Eve," the magic teacher stated, "Come along. You've got much to learn and others to see."

The little psychic hesitated as she removed her wrists from the restraints. She rubbed them as she meekly answered, "I'm not sure if I want to leave here. I've hurt others. People I don't know that brought me here. I doubt that they would want to see me, let alone be friends."

"You'll never know until you give it a chance. People that come here tend to be banged up and not in a right state of mind. Many have died from their trauma from the Reset, while others like yourself, have survived. It may take a while, but you will find a certain kinship with the residents of the facility. Trust me when I say that you've had other visitors checking in on you while you slept and recovered."

Eve stood up and her stomach growled. She sheepishly grabbed the sandwich and the glass of wine. She never drank alcohol before, but it seemed rude if she let it go to waste, especially if what Adoy said about the woman was true.

Her new magical teacher opened the door and waved his arm out at it and said, "Come, child. Your new life begins now."

Chapter Twelve

Eve walked down the hallway, going nowhere in particular. She just finished a long training session with Adoy and was famished. She knew that she should eat something, but didn't want to bother anyone about it.

Adoy told her more about the Reset and what was happening outside these cold walls during the time she spent with him. He also explained that the ley lines that were once dormant were now supercharged, which is why her abilities were so active and out of control. Eve wasn't sure if it was true or if it was a failure on her part.

The thought of leaving this place terrified the little psychic. Who in their right mind would attempt it? Plenty, she found out as more raiding teams went to and from the facility. They tirelessly hunted for more people like herself, the gifted ones.

People were still killing themselves and others were attacking anyone or anything that moved. Eve shuttered, recalling what happened to her at the state hospital. If she hadn't experienced it first hand, Eve wouldn't have believed it.

She was lost in her thoughts when she heard someone clear their throat. She turned her head and saw Moneek standing nearby. At first, her face blanched. She thought he was her personal tormentor, which wasn't possible here. Her magical teacher told her of the different wards and enchantments on the facility that kept the negative entities at bay. Eve wanted to believe that Moneek was different, but he was a demon.

"I'm glad to see that you're up and about now. I hated seeing you all tied up like that." Moneek stated as he approached. He saw Eve's face and added, "I'm not him, you know. I'm not going to hurt you, Eve."

The little psychic shrugged her shoulders as she walked away. She hoped that the demon would get the hint and leave, but he fell in step beside her. Moneek looked at her and asked, "When's the last time you had a decent meal?"

"Why do you care?" Eve muttered.

"You look famished and I can see that you're exhausted. So, tell me?"

"Meg gave me a sandwich and a glass of wine earlier. Does that count?"

Moneek grunted and shook his head, "That witch and her wine. No, it doesn't. When was your last real substantial meal?"

Eve shrugged her shoulders as she rubbed her arm, "The hospital."

"Oh dear, that won't do. You need food, Eve. I can take you-"

Eve turned and growled at the demon, catching him by surprise. The little psychic poked him on his chest and said, "You're not my keeper! I can take care of myself just fine. I may be a pathetic girl, but I'm a survivor. I'm not helpless, you know!"

"I never said you were. I'm not *him*, damn it!" Moneek huffed as he watched her intently. She swayed as her body trembled. "Come along, Eve. Let's get some food in your belly so you won't pass out."

As he reached for her, Eve yanked her arm back like she was avoiding the strike of a viper. Moneek grumbled as he stated, "Fine. You want to do this the hard way, that can be arranged."

The demon teleported himself behind the little psychic and wrapped his arms around her. She struggled for a moment and then, everything went black. Eve felt bile threatening to unleash along with the little contents of her stomach. She glared at the demon, but he wasn't paying attention as he spoke to someone else, "Porta, Eve is in need of a hot meal. Can you whip something up for her?"

"Sure," the magical chef countered with a glare, "but I'd rather she walk in here on her own. People who aren't used to teleporting tend to get sick. I don't like having to clean up *your* messes."

Moneek looked away as he apologized, his cheeks heating up, "Sorry, but it's an emergency. Ms. Driskell hasn't had a decent meal in five days. If she spews, I swear that I will clean it up, just help her. I beg you."

Porta harrumphed as she crossed her arms against her chest, "She needs to order before I can do as you asked, Moneek. I'm not a mind reader, you know."

Eve peeked around the demon to see who he was talking to. As soon as they locked eyes in each other, Porta's irritation melted away. She came from behind the counter to examine the little psychic, "Oh honey, I hope you don't think I'm mad at you." She gently pulled her away from Moneek to a nearby table, "You sit down here and tell Porta what you want to eat."

"I'm okay, ma'am," Eve shrugged her shoulders as she rubbed her arm, "Meg gave me a sandwich and some wine earlier."

"That was for you? I thought it was for her. Meg loves her wine so I didn't think anything of it."

Eve looked down at the table and muttered, "I don't want to put you out. I should just go. You've already fed me. I-I don't want to be a bother."

Porta's mouth opened, surprised at the girl's attitude. She clamped her mouth shut as she put a hand on her shoulder. Determined to feed the little psychic, the chef said, "it's Eve, isn't it?" When she slightly nodded, Porta continued, "I'm the chef of this facility so it's not only my job to feed the residents here, but it's my magical talent. I can make anything that your little heart desires. Do tell me what you want?"

"Bread and water will suffice."

"Eve," Porta replied, feeling a little irritated by the request because she could magically see that the girl was dangerously in need of food, "that's not a meal. Trust me when I say that you can have anything you want. No matter what. No money is required here."

"Why do any of you care what happens to me?" Eve harshly bit out as she crossed her arms on the table and buried her face against the surface, crying as her body spasmed, "I'm just a good for nothing freakshow! Feed someone else who deserves it more than me.

I'm worthless and weak in every aspect and not to be trusted."

"Who filled your head with all those mean things?" Porta asked.

"A demon did, so it must be true."

The chef glared at Moneek, "People coming in here are traumatized enough. Did you say this about her?"

He put his hands up, pleading, "It wasn't me! She has another demon bound to her. That's who she's referring to. I would never hurt her like he did, honestly."

Eve felt a hand rubbing her back and heard a familiar female voice speak to her, "Eve, you need to eat. Your demon buddy isn't here. Stop the pity party and let this woman feed you. Why did you come into the cafeteria if you weren't going to eat?"

She looked up at Jayne and corrected, "I didn't come here. I was brought here against my will. It seems like that's everyone's goal for me. Making me do whatever they think is best for me. Just use your magic and kill me. I don't want to be a burden anymore."

"You're not being a burden, more like a little brat!" Red Jayne hissed as she threw her hands up in the air, "I just don't get you, Eve. You're no longer in the state hospital, your demon can't get to you in here. Why the fuck are you going to shit?"

"Enough, my dear!" Fal grumbled as he put a hand on Jayne's shoulder, "I've watched over her for a while. You don't know her full story. Eve has every reason to believe it because many people have torn her down."

"Maybe so, but it doesn't give her license to shit on those trying to help her sorry, ungrateful ass! What makes her so special?"

Fal sat down next to Porta, "You're correct, Jayne, but we aren't here to keep tearing her down like those that came before us. She needs friends and compassion, not more negativity."

"Whose life hasn't been rough? I didn't have a wonderful childhood. You don't see me crying about it like a baby! She needs to suck it up and move forward, not wallowing in her miserable past."

Eve sat up and tried to leave, but before she could get to the door, she collapsed. Despite this, the little psychic attempted to crawl away. Moneek leaned down and turned her over onto her back.

"This is why I brought you here. You need food and more rest. If you eat, can I take you back to your room?"

Jayne walked by and out of the cafeteria, muttering, "Drama queen."

"I can get to my room without your help," Eve bit out as she attempted to free herself from the demon's grasp, but couldn't. She didn't have the energy to fight. "Just toss me out into the cold outside and let nature take its course."

"Boys she needs to see Dr Arnica." The chef stated with alarm in her voice. She hurried over to a phone on the wall.

"No, I don't. I promise that I'm not a threat to you or myself. I'll be good, I swear! Don't lock me up again!" Eve cried out, pleading to anyone who would listen. Fal stood over her with his arms clasped behind his back, showing little emotion. Moneek pleaded with her, "It's not like that at all, Eve. No one's locking you up nor is anyone going to toss you out to die. This is a safe place. We're all here for you, if you let us. I don't like seeing you like this. It breaks my heart."

"Demons don't have a heart!" Eve bit out as she shook her head, "There's no such thing as a *good* demon."

"That's true, but like everything, there are exceptions." Fal stated calmly, "Moneek and his people live in a secret domain, hidden from others like them because they found a way not to feed off negativity. He legitimately doesn't want to hurt you, like the one who tricked you all those years ago."

A puff of air gusted over Eve's face as a pale female stood there. She spoke to the chef with a thick southern drawl, "I'm here. What is the situation, Porta?"

"Eve's in need of medical care, Gloria! The magic within her is sapping her bad. She needs bed rest and no more use of her magic. Food too, but she needs better care."

"Say no more, my old friend," the vampire said as she leaned down and effortlessly lifted the little psychic up, cradling her tightly, "Keep up, demon. I'm not letting this one die under my protection. Close your eyes, child. My speed could affect you, so hold on."

The little psychic felt a rush of air blasting against her, like she was riding a motorcycle, but at twice the speed. She focused on the woman's face as the whole world flew by in a blur. Her face was unmarred and youthful, but her skin was pale. Gloria's thick blonde hair freely fluttered about, like they were in a photoshoot.

The vampire glanced down and said, "I have you. Don't fear me."

Eve gulped, her anxiety rising, "I'm... I'm not afraid of you."

"Yes, you are. You just don't realize why. I can smell it coming out of you like incense."

"What does my fear smell like?"

She watched as Gloria's eyes changed from hazel to crimson red, "Delicious, my child. Don't worry, I won't bite you."

"If you do, kill me," Eve muttered as she held on tighter.

Gloria eyed the little psychic, "Is that an invitation?"

"For death? Yes."

Gloria stopped suddenly by a red metal door. She reached to open it, but Moneek opened it up from inside, "You're getting slow, Gloria. It felt like I was waiting in here forever."

"It wasn't a race, you sulphur scented simp! Move aside so I can put her on a bed."

"No beds available. All full from another raid. Dr Arnica wants her in her own room. She sent Jace to prep it."

The vampire nodded, "Where's her room located?"

"She's staying in my room, for the time being." He looked at Eve and saw that her eyes held fear, "I need time with her to see if I can break whatever connections the other demon has on her. If I can figure them out, then it will make it difficult for him to track her down."

"She's terrified of this plan. I suspect that you didn't make her privy to it until now." The female vampire glared at the demon.

"I wanted to," Moneek shuffled from foot to foot, "but I didn't get a chance. She needed food because she was so shaky. I didn't realize that her power was causing this."

"Do you want to stay with him? You can bunk with me instead, Eve?"

"Like I have a choice," Eve muttered. "Do whatever you want to me, I'm a punching bag for everyone in my life."

Eve felt the vampire turn and sped off; the scent of metallic peaches assailed her nostrils. She wondered if everyone here bathed with different soaps or was wearing perfume. The little psychic could hear the woman's thoughts, but she was genuinely surprised by what she heard.

"She reminds me of my child when I was a mortal. Precious little spark of life. Never fade, not again."

Gloria stopped abruptly at a brown metal door. It was open most of the way, the vampire saw Jace working tirelessly at prepping the room. She cleared her throat as she stepped inside, "Coming in, Jace."

Gloria gently placed Eve onto the bed. Before she turned to leave, the little psychic grasped her hand and said, "What was your child's name?"

"How did you know about her?" Gloria narrowed her gaze on the little psychic, causing her to avert her eyes.

"I heard you thinking. That I reminded you of your child. You also said precious little spark of life. I'm sorry, I didn't mean to pry. "

"Another story for another time. I will tell you about it, if you can heal up."

"Were you referring to me or your child not to fade away again?"

The vampire leaned down and pulled the blanket over Eve's body, tucking her in. Gloria pressed her lips against Eve's forehead and replied, "Let us help, Eve. Don't let your fears and paranoia keep you from getting better. Promise me, child. I don't want to dig another grave."

Eve slowly nodded, "I promise to behave. I'm not going to hurt myself or others. What are you, Gloria?"

Gloria stood up and smiled at her, like a matriarch of a family could, "A friend. One that will tell more if you can heal. I want to see you when you're able and ready. Deal?"

"It's a deal, Gloria. I'll do my best not to let you down."

"You *never* have and you never will..." The vampire cryptically uttered as she sped out of the room.

Chapter Thirteen

Eve looked over at Jace. He was young, maybe in his twenties, like herself. When he moved around the bed, Eve caught the scent of spearmint.

"Does everyone here wear perfume? Everyone smells different." Eve asked.

He looked at the little psychic as he hooked up a saline solution on an IV rack, "No, not that I know of. I've heard that everyone has a unique scent that they produce. I've smelled it, like you do and yet, I have no idea if I do it or not."

He picked up her arm and wrapped a rubber tourniquet tightly against her bicep. Eve nervously nibbled on the inside of her cheek as she asked, "Do I have one? An odor?"

Jace smiled brightly, "I'll tell you if you do the same for me in return."

She yelped as he inserted the IV needle into her vein just below the bend at the elbow. She looked into his sapphire eyes and said, "Spearmint. That's what I smell."

"At least it's pleasant," the healer quipped, "I figured that I smelled like a box of Band-Aids."

Eve couldn't stifle the giggles that erupted from her mouth. He lifted her hand up to his nose and inhaled deeply, causing the little psychic's stomach to flutter with anticipation.

"Roses. It's fitting for you, Eve." Jace said before leaving the room with the smile.

Eve smiled as she saw a woman in a white lab coat enter the room, along with Adoy, Moneek, Meg, and Red Jayne. The doctor sat down on the bed, listening to Eve's heart as Adoy spoke, "She shouldn't be in this condition. What does your third eye see?"

Meg gasped, "It looks like she's losing energy, like something is sucking it out."

"How is this possible," the magical teacher asked.

"It feels like she's somehow tapped into a ley line," Red Jayne stated, feeling bewildered, "That's not possible for her, is it?"

"Ley lines can be accessed by anyone with the right skills and knowledge. I fear that there's more going on than we realize." Adoy commented. He turned and looked at Moneek, "What do you see, demon?"

"It's not natural. Someone is doing it to her. It needs to be severed, at once!"

Eve kept blinking her eyes, wanting to go to sleep and never wake up. Dr Arnica turned and shouted, "Her heart beat is slow and erratic. If something isn't done, she'll die."

"No!" Moneek cried out as he squatted next to the bed, "Help me save her, Red!"

Red Jayne moved over and sat down on the bed next to the demon. Meg wedged herself between the two, grounding into the Earth. Eve opened her eyes and saw everyone by her side, hands at the edge of touching her body. Meg calmly stated, "Touch me and use the energy to help fight off her attacker."

Red Jayne complied, but warned, "You could die if this goes south."

"Fuck that and do it right then," Meg snapped, "You too, demon. I'm not about to let

173

some fucking parasite kill my new friend. If she goes, I'm going too. She's worth the risk!"

Moneek put his hand on the witch's shoulder and pointed at the little psychic's chest, "The source is there, Red! Break it!"

The energy worker reached out her hand, trying to grasp the invasive bond. She grunted painfully as she spat, "It's too strong! I might kill her with the backlash of ley line energy! Meg, juice up. You need to be a fountain and a buffer for this to work!"

"Don't have to tell me twice," Meg gritted as her body flooded with the natural energy of the Earth. Meg's body hummed as power coursed through her, strands of her silky black hair flowed in the air. Moneek placed his hand on top of Eve's heart. He dug his claws into the bond, grimacing from the raw power that seemed to beg for his energy too.

"He's bridged a bond into a ley line, the bastard! Break it, Jayne!" The demon cried out.

"Brace for the feedback, Meg!" Jayne commanded as she gripped the bond and crushed the link in her hand and pushed it into the witch. A wave of magic flung everyone away from the bed. An ethereal voice echoed maliciously in the room, causing Eve to cower, "*You may have stopped me this time, but I will claim my pupil. One way or another...*"

Meg moaned as she was sprawled on her back, "Help me get...to Eve!"

The demon and Adoy assisted the witch up. She collapsed her weight on Eve's legs. Their eyes met as she bit out, "Take it and feel better, little miss know-it-all."

"I accept," Eve replied as energy coursed throughout her body from the witch. Meg's body spasmed and lurched, but she refused to let her body off of Eve.

Eve cried, tears streaming down her face, "Don't die for me! I'm not worth it!"

Meg grinned like a mad woman at the little psychic, "I'm not letting you go out like a demon's little bitch! When I find him, I'm going to present his head to you like a trophy! Damn, this hurts so bad!" She buried her face on the blanket, crying.

The witch felt a timid hand on her arm. She glanced over and saw Eve staring back at her, "Let go, Meg."

"Easier. Said. Than. Done." Meg croaked, feeling overwhelmed by the raw power. Adoy commanded as he placed his tiny hands on Meg's back, "Help push the energy back in the Earth. I'll unground her."

Eve looked on, clueless about how to help the witch. The little psychic barely knew the woman and yet, she had no problem risking her life for her. Meg groaned as the power drained away through her roots, her breathing came in rapid succession.

The witch shivered as she felt her grounding roots curl back inside her body. She lulled her head to the side, eyeing the little psychic, "No one messes with my friends. Feel better, Eve?"

"Me? What about you?"

"Magic always comes with a price. I'd gladly pay it for any of you." Meg stated before passing out. Moneek picked up the witch and said, "I'll put her to bed. Mia can watch over her, if need be."

"Careful, the shifter might get pissed when she finds out what happened," Red Jayne warned.

"I'll accept anything that the wolf dishes out. It's my fault that I couldn't keep Eve safe," he said solemnly before teleporting away. Adoy walked over and placed a hand on Eve as the doctor reexamined her.

"How do you feel, Ms. Driskell?" He asked.

"Weird. Tired but energized at the same time. She- is Meg going to be okay?"

"It's nothing that she can't handle. The witch is quite resilient, much like yourself."

Dr Arnica stood up and stated, "You need bed rest and fluids. Something you should've gotten since coming here. That's on me, but it's not an excuse. I'm the only doctor here and I'm failing to save lives."

"If you can spare Jace at some point, I'll teach him how to use his natural healing talents. You will need more healers on your team and that will hopefully alleviate some of the burden on you."

"I'd appreciate it, but I don't know if he has the time. The more wounded that come in, the less time any of us in medical have."

"I'd like to learn, if it's okay," Jayne asked, "Maybe you can teach me. Maybe I can use my energy work to heal others."

Adoy looked at her and thought about it, "Park the ego and be more selfless. Those are my conditions. If you can't, I won't waste my time, even though you're talented with energy work. If you learn from me, you *will* be expected to teach others. That's how we can get through this."

Eve watched as the energy worker slumped her shoulders and nodded, "I accept your terms, Adoy. If Meg has taught me anything, it's that she's ready to help others that need it." She looked at the little psychic and added, "I'm sorry Eve. I'm sorry for giving you so much grief since we got here."

"You're frustrated with the stress of the Reset. I can see it clearly in your mind." The little psychic replied.

"That's not an excuse for being a bitch!" Jayne snapped, causing Eve to flinch, "I'm sorry! I'll- I need to get some air. I'm glad you're okay."

Jayne stormed out of the room, brushing past Fal and the demon as they entered the room. The fae warrior looked on and asked, "How is she doing?"

"Better. She needs rest. One of you see to it that her needs are tended to," Dr Arnica ordered.

"I'm sure that can be arranged," Fal'destion stated, "Anything else you require?"

"More doctors, nurses, and healers would be great!" The doctor bit out, "Maybe see if some of the teams can raid the different hospitals and clinics for more supplies?"

"I'll go now and see if I can recruit aides for you, doctor. In the name of my Goddess Moonrose, you *will* get what you need."

"Thanks," Dr Arnica said, but the fae warrior was already out the door. She looked at the demon. He shrugged his shoulders, "Fal isn't one that minced words. If anyone can get you the support you requested, it's him."

"Make sure that she eats. Fluids can only do so much for her," Dr Arnica ordered.

"Yes, doctor. I'll stay and watch over her."

"That's not necessary," Eve protested, "I feel better. I don't need a chaperone."

"No, Eve." The doctor admonished, "Rest now and we'll talk about it tomorrow."

The demon grabbed a chair and sat down by her bedside as the doctor left the room. A strong whiff of strawberries assailed her nostrils as the little psychic inhaled. Moneek leaned forward, his forearms resting on his thighs, "What can I get you, food wise?"

"You don't have to get me anything. I can walk there, you know."

The demon eyed her, "Where is the cafeteria exactly?" Eve shrugged her shoulders so Moneek continued, "This place is huge and one can get turned around and lost. You need rest, not aimlessly wandering the halls."

Eve rubbed her arm as she looked down at the IV, "Why do you care? Don't you have someone else to torture?"

"That's not what I do, Eve," Moneek grunted with frustration, "Me and my people learned how to live off positive things, like love and happiness."

"Uh huh. I guess that makes you better than other demons?"

"Have I done anything to warrant your despise and mistrust?" The demon asked as he stood up.

"Not yet, but I'm sure that it's only a matter of time before you find a way to humiliate me or hurt me. Everyone seems to do it in the end."

"I'm not *him*!" Moneek growled. When he saw her flinch, he pinched the bridge of his nose and sighed, "I'm sorry. I'm so tired of others judging me because of what I am. I understand completely. To my kind, we're outcasts. If they knew where my people lived, they'd eradicate us. You have your fears of demons, which are valid. Just don't lump me in that group. Now, what do you want to eat?"

Eve shrugged her shoulders, still not looking at him, "I truly don't know. That's partly why I asked for bread and water. It's something that I ate because that was all I could afford at times. I don't want to be a burden on others. I have no clue what the chef has available."

The demon chuckled, which both irritated and caused the little psychic to smile. She finally turned her head and asked, "What's so funny? She didn't have a menu for the day's special." Moneek cackled louder, holding his belly as the Eve growled, "Stop it. It isn't funny. Why are you making fun of me?"

He held up a clawed hand as tears streamed down his demonic visage, "I'm not making fun of you. I thought the same thing when I first met Porta. Oh my, was I a fool. It didn't dawn on me that she was a being not of this world. She surprised me when she made me food that can't be made here on Earth. The ingredients don't come from here. She gave me quite the lecture that day, but also told me that she can make anything. I'm a believer now. That said, what is your favorite meal of all time?"

Eve barely smiled as she thought for a moment, "You're sure that she can make anything? If not-"

"I bet my life on it. I have a knife that you can plunge into my heart. Come on, Eve. It's the apocalypse, baby. Roll with it. Porta lives to serve food and she's talented. She has no menu because she uses magic to create your order and she's been around for centuries."

Eve's mouth gaped, "She doesn't look that old. She looks like she's in her forties. I'm not anyone's baby!" Eve felt like it was a lie for some reason, so she decided to be bold and ask, "You never said why you care. Why do you?"

The demon slowly reached out and caressed the back of his fingers against her soft cheek. He spoke softly, "Everyone deserves a chance at love and to feel loved. You more than deserve both. I'm not the bad guy here, I just want to keep you safe from the real enemy."

Eve nodded. It felt strange that she seemed to enjoy his touch. It confused her because when her tormentor touched her in any way, it caused revulsion. With Moneek, Eve didn't react that way. He seemed to be genuine and sincere, but the little psychic was on the precipice on the matter.

Am I being too hard on him?

"Fine. I'll tell you, but I'm sure that you'll think it's strange."

Moneek grabbed a pen and a small paper tablet, grinning ear to ear, "I highly doubt it. What's a common cuisine to me would be strange to you, if you saw it."

Eve muttered her order, feeling self-conscious about it. The demon eyed her as he said, "Care to repeat it a little louder?"

"A ham and cheese omelet with biscuits and... chocolate gravy."

"Got it. Anything to drink, baby?" Moneek calmly asked.

Eve expected him to laugh or mock her choice, but it didn't happen. She gulped, not sure what to make of this demon.

"Lemonade and... why do you think that I deserve anything, especially love?" The little psychic asked as she held her breath, waiting for him to answer.

He scribbled her order on the paper and looked at her with a possessive stare, "Why wouldn't you? I'd gladly slay a thousand demons without batting an eye if it meant that you could've a chance for happiness, safety, and love. I know that you see me in a different light. I hope that I can earn your trust one day. I can patiently wait while helping you learn more about your talents, though I believe Fal can do better."

Eve slightly blushed, "You're not mad at me?"

Moneek snorted, "For not trusting demons? I would like to say that it's the sensible thing to do. I'd think you were mad if you didn't."

"That's debatable since I turned fifteen. I've seen and heard things that no one else could." Eve slumped her shoulders, "I guess that I am a mad woman."

"Nonsense. You're far from it. In fact, the Reset, in a way, has validated everything you've experienced thus far. Madness is what the Ferals are and you're not one of them. If anything, you were more suited for this. Now, if you'll excuse me. I have a sweet, not-so-crazy, I told you so woman to feed."

The demon winked before teleporting away. The little psychic shook her head as she stood up and walked towards the bathroom, dragging her IV stand beside her. She sat down on the toilet thinking about her conversation with Moneek as she did her business.

Did it matter that Moneek was a demon?

It did. She rubbed her eyes as another thought occurred to her. *Do I deserve love and happiness?* Eve wasn't sure what those were. She barely remembered what her childhood was like, those simpler times. Ever since her fifteenth birthday, life was Hell on a daily basis. Her tormentor gleefully saw to it.

Eve heard a quick knock on the wall outside of the bathroom. Her stomach demandingly growled at the prospect of food. The little psychic wiped her lady parts and flushed the toilet, saying with a smile, "I'll be out in a minute."

She washed her hands and wiped them on her shirt. Eve opened the door and was met by the fae warrior, her smile wavered. She stepped out and meekly walked over to her bed, "Hi, Fal. Did you need something from me?"

"What I need from you is to get better. I want to help train you. I feel like it's in your best interest to learn more fighting styles."

"Am I expected to do this? What makes any of you think that I want to?" Eve asked as she wrapped her arms around her chest. Fal watched her quietly for a few minutes before stating, "War is coming and you need to learn how to properly fight. There may be times when your gifts won't protect you."

"The moment I set foot outside of this place, I'm dead. *He* will come for me. *He* always does..." Eve answered, her eyes vacant.

Fal grumbled to himself and then he caught the little psychic by surprise. The fae warrior smiled. "We can use it to our advantage."

Eve wasn't liking where this conversation was going, "What do you mean by that?"

"If we can lure your demon out into the open, then we can end his pathetic existence. You wouldn't have to be worrying about him coming to harm you if he's dead."

"He might be dead. The Ferals could have killed him." Eve offered hopefully.

Fal eyed her, "From what I heard, he's alive and well and just tried to kill you. Demons are hard to kill so don't count on the crazed fools outside to end him for you."

"I don't want to be a piece of cheese for this trap," Eve said as Moneek reappeared by her bedside. He sat the tray of food on her bed. Fal stepped forward and looked down at it and asked, "Is that chocolate?"

Eve grinned as she poured the chocolate gravy over the biscuits, "Yes, it is. Do you want some?"

"No," he muttered softly, "just curious. Do you eat chocolate on everything or just this bread?"

She used a fork to cut a piece of the biscuit off and swirled it in the gravy before sticking it into her mouth. Eve's eyes rolled back in her head as she let out a moan of pleasure, "This taste so good! I can't believe that it has been so long since I had this. My grandmother used to make this for me when I was a little girl."

Fal watched as the little psychic teared up and asked, "What's wrong? What's troubling you, child?"

"Too many fond memories. This actually tastes better than my grandmother's version. I didn't think it was possible."

"Porta is an excellent chef," the demon replied, "So feel free to order whatever you wish and if anyone gives you grief about what food you eat, let her know and she will deal with them harshly. Her words, not mine."

"No arguments. The proof is on my plate," Eve smiled as she ate a bite of the omelet. She wasn't sure how, but the eggs were firm and silky, the ham was salty and crunchy, and the cheese was gooey and rich like the chocolate gravy. Eve took a sip of the lemonade and offered some to the fae warrior.

Fal backed away with a hand up, "No, it's for you. I can't have it because it has lemons in it."

Eve glanced at the demon and then back at Fal, "Are you allergic to lemons?"

"You could say that," Fal replied, "Lemons are deadly to the Fae. If I drank it, it would be excruciatingly painful. It would kill me eventually."

The little psychic sat the cup down. She looked down at her food, rubbing her arm, "I'm sorry. I didn't mean to threaten you with it."

The fae warrior shrugged his shoulders slightly, "You didn't know, so there's no reason to apologize. Eat your meal and rest."

The fae warrior turned on his heels and marched out of the room. Eve silently ate her meal as the demon sat on the chair, watching her.

Chapter Fourteen

After several days of bed rest, Eve finally got the okay from the doctor to move about freely. During the next few weeks, Fal kept taking Eve outside to help acclimate her to the outside world and possibly lure out her tormentor. She got around to meeting the other people in the facility, despite not wanting to. Moneek and Fal insisted on it, arguing that it was in her best interest because she needed to make positive connections.

Eve had difficulty focusing, most of the residents weren't shielding their thoughts. She didn't blame them for it. It was something that she had to manage.

They shouldn't have to change just for me, the little psychic thought. Her *gifts,* as everyone seemed to refer to her psychic abilities, was her burden to carry. She walked in one of the training rooms and found the fae warrior, patiently waiting for her. The room had other people training with weapons or magic. She saw the witch looking at her, smiling and waving at the little psychic.

Eve's lips barely lifted with a smile as she quickly waved back. Why Meg liked her, Eve couldn't say. The witch accepted her for who she was and didn't care about her past, something that the little psychic wasn't used to having in her short life.

The witch was talking to some of the other people, she had taken her role as a magical teacher in stride. Meg was preparing to spar with a cocky, ebony skin young man who went by the name Black Jack.

A slight grunt drew Eve's attention to the fae warrior. She could never tell what he was thinking, let alone what he was feeling emotionally. He came off as cold and aloof. He told her that he was taught from a young age how to master not only his emotional state, but his tolerance for pain.

"Are you ready to begin, child?" The fae warrior asked, his voice calm and devoid of emotion.

"I think so. Why does everyone keep calling me a child?"

"Compared to them, myself included, you are."

Eve gaze fell on Fal'destion's facial features, not seeing any blemishes or other signs of aging, "You're not *that* much older than me, are you?"

"My kind doesn't age at the same rate as humans." The fae warrior replied, the corners of his lips lifted slightly, "You maybe an adult, but to me you're a baby. I'm over seven hundred years old, Ms. Driskell."

She gasped, "No way! You don't look much older than me."

Fal slightly shrugged his shoulders, "Let's begin. Attack my defenses."

Eve nodded, the lingering fear of hurting the fae warrior crept up from the dark reaches of her mind. Fal explained to her that she needed a difficult target to practice her psychic abilities. It's one thing to attack a novice mind than one with layers of protections in place. Fal seemed confident that she could do it and not to worry about causing him harm.

Eve didn't have the same hope about herself as he did. *Why do so many strangers that don't know me feel this way about me,* Eve thought as she focused on the fae warrior in front of her.

"*Because you can,*" a familiar female voice spoke softly in her mind, "*To them, you shine like a beacon of hope and survival. You don't realize how much that means to people during difficult times. You're a savior to those that have experienced trauma and pain. A gentle hand of support.*"

Eve probed Fal's mental barriers, finding it difficult to scratch as she mentally replied, "*I'm not that person. I'm a worthless piece of crap that can't manage my powers, let alone, my mental health. I've not done anything for any of these kind people, of the sort.*"

"*In time, Eve, you will understand what I mean.*" The Protector stated, "*Now, stop attacking yourself and focus on your training.*"

The little psychic curtly nodded. She grimaced as she pushed more psychic energy at the fae warrior's barrier. He squinted his eyes, but didn't budge as she kept adding pressure. Eve gasped as she could no longer sustain her assault on Fal. She leaned down and grabbed her knees, panting, as the fae warrior walked over to her.

"Good attempt, Eve. I felt the pressure, but you need to be more precise if you wish to succeed."

Eve rubbed her arm meekly as she stood up straight, "I'm not sure how?"

"You're using brute force. Not all attacks require it. Finesse and patience can yield better results."

"What do you mean, Fal?" Eve sighed as she looked at her feet, shaking her head, "My ignorance will be my downfall. I guess my first teacher was right about me. Stupid girl."

"Nonsense," Fal snapped, causing her to look at him. She never heard him raise his voice with such anger. It shocked the little psychic, just as much as how he went back to being aloof, "He only used you for his own gains. You learned pain and suffering, not how to properly use your gifts. Ignorance can be destroyed by knowledge. Your imagination is your only limitation when it comes to magic."

"Huh?"

Fal nudged Eve to walk with him as Mia strolled by them, heading straight for her witch, "Magic resides in all of us. It's like an extension of yourself. If not properly trained and honed, it manifests itself in many ways, like how you were when we came for you. The demon gave you just enough knowledge to keep you in check. Had he taught you more, I suspect that he worried that you wouldn't need him and might actually stand up to him. Demons prefer to feed off negativity, which is why he hurt you so often."

"So, if I think of using my psychic powers like a jackhammer on your barrier, it will do it?" Eve smiled playfully.

"Yes, but that goes back to using brute force. Think of it as delicate work, like how your scientists would take time and care in unearthing fossils and relics of the past. You don't want to destroy the contents of what's hidden from you."

Eve nodded as they heard Mia announced, "We have a job to do. Get prepped, we go in twenty minutes."

Meg paled slightly, "Am I coming on this one?"

"Yes," Mia stated as she barked out, "Jack! Victor and Axel will be accompanying us downtown, they're stocking a vehicle with the necessary equipment. Get geared up, sorcerer. Meet us in the garage."

Meg bit her bottom lip, suddenly feeling the need to escape. The witch hadn't set foot outside the walls of the facility. Eric materialized beside her and stated, *"You're paler than me, witch... What's scaring you...?"*

"What're you talking about, dude," Jack asked, "Meg's a badass witch with a mean streak. Nothing scares her!" He looked at Meg and wearily added with concern, "Right, Meg?"

Before Mia could reach her, Meg bolted out of the training room, not caring if anyone was following her. She vaguely heard her name being called, but sounded hollow and distant. *Training was one thing*, the witch thought, *fighting what's beyond the walls was entirely different.*

Eve looked at Fal and said, "I must go to her. She needs my help."

"I had a feeling that you would say that," the fae warrior answered as they both bolted out of the training room. The little psychic could feel everyone's thoughts, the pressure and the chaotic voices screaming painfully in her head. She felt Fal's hand wrap around her petite body, supporting her. They stopped as they rounded the corner, watching Meg collide into Moneek. The witch fell down onto the floor, Eve could feel the intensity of Meg's panic.

"Dear me, what's with the running around like a rabbit being hunted? Someone could get hurt. Here, let me- "

"I'm fine," the witch spat as she scrambled to her feet. The creature grabbed her by the arm, stopping her as Mia, Jack and Eve caught up.

"Let me go! I have something I need to do!"

"Meg, what gives?" Jack asked, feeling confused.

"Is it Axel?" Mia snarled, "Has he threatened you again?"

"No, nothing like that," Meg replied, still trying to free herself from the entity's grip.

"I swear I didn't do this to her," the crimson creature spoke, not liking how the shifter was eyeing him, "She ran into me. I'm merely trying to aid this rude lady."

"She's scared," Mia roared. She pulled the witch into her arms as the creature let go. "I'm trying to figure out what's got her all worked up."

"I'm fine," Meg growled at everyone, "Why won't you leave me alone?"

Chapter Fifteen

Eve grimaced as she moved purposefully towards the witch. She did her best to shield her mind from sponging up every thought around her, but she knew it wouldn't last. This gave her the courage to make her way to Meg. She *had* to do it. *Meg needs me, now more than ever. I hope I don't fail her.*

The witch felt a timid hand on her shoulder. She knew who it was without even looking, but she did. Meg's eyes were full of fear as she looked at Eve, who said, "She's afraid to go out."

"Meg ain't afraid of nothing, girl!" Black Jack answered. He pointed at the witch, "She can toss me around and bring Axel to his knees, begging for mercy. What can she possibly be afraid of.?"

Eve turned to look deadpan at the sorcerer, coldly uttered, "You know of trauma, do you?"

"Who doesn't? Everyone here's been through some shit. What does it matter?" Black Jack replied, exasperated.

Moneek backed away from the group, putting its hands up, "I'm no threat, Meg. Eve, speak to her please? I know you can-"

"Reach her? Be a lifeline, in her time of need? She has a *mate* that can do that for her, *demon*?" Eve hissed.

"Why are you backing away, Moneek?" Mia asked.

"Oh, Gods!" Meg cried out, trying to free herself from Mia's hold, her eyes wildly darted everywhere, "Why aren't you listening to me? Let me go!"

"She's a powerful witch, caught up in a PTSD moment," The demon replied as he moved out of Meg's view, "Do you think that I want to be her target when she's ready to fight? I'm good, thank you."

"No good demons exist," Eve muttered, knowing that Moneek could hear her. "It's her first time being told to leave this place."

Bewildered, the shifter shook her head, "What? No one told her to leave!"

"It's what she believes," Eve shrugged her shoulders.

"The mission?" Black Jack stroked his chin, "Do you think that is what caused this little freak out?"

"Did she know about it, the mission?" The psychic asked the shifter.

"No, I didn't know about the mission until ten minutes ago. Did..." Mia gulped as she held the witch against her warm body, "Are you saying that *I* caused this?"

Eve backed away as the shifter's eyes glowed, "Trauma is different for everyone. You need to reassure her that she's safe. Meg's ready to blow a hole in the walls until she can find a way out of here. She's terrified and not in the right frame of mind to do anything."

"She can't go on the mission like this," the demon piped up from around the corner, "I can go in her stead, Mia."

"But who will go in my place?" Mia asked, her emotions warred across her visage. She was the one in charge of the mission, she had to go. Yet, the shifter was torn. She wanted to take the witch back to her room and hold her until she calmed down.

"Allow me to take care of her." Eve stated. The shifter eyed the psychic, causing her to look at her feet in shame, "I know much about what she's going through."

"*You* think that I can't save her?" Mia snarled, causing the psychic to flinch.

"No, I don't," Eve meekly stated, "You see her as though she's in danger and all you want to do is find the closest threat to her because of your wolf nature. That's not what she needs and deep down, you know. I'm not a threat to you or her."

"I don't like this," Mia grumbled.

"It's not about you, it's about her and what she needs. Meg is a rude and gruff witch, but she showed me a kindness when I got here. She's been hard, but good to me. Let me return a favor?" Eve pleaded her case.

"Stop talking about me like I'm not here, damnit!" Meg demanded as the shifter let her go. She glared at everyone as she slowly turned in a circle, her magic thrumming and at her command. "Do you think that I'm a weak idiot? I love it here and you'll *not* be taking my home from me again!"

"Meg, no one is doing that," Mia answered as tears streamed down her face.

Eve sat down on the cold concrete floor with her head pressed against her knees, crying. The witch looked down at the psychic, wondering what was happening to her. She kneeled down by her as she rubbed her back, "Don't tell me that they're kicking you out too?"

"No," Eve bit out between sobs, "Emotional overload. Too. Much. To. Bear."

Meg grabbed the psychic protectively and commanded, "Step back. She's hearing us all!"

Everyone moved back, hoping it would help, as Mia replied, "Mental shielding up! You too, Meg!"

The witch nodded as she focused on building an impenetrable barrier in her mind's eye. She noticed that her emotions were all over the place and now felt bad for Eve.

She shouldn't have to suffer because I got lazy.

"*You're not lazy,*" Eve mentally spoke to the witch, "*It's my fault I'm like this. Don't feel bad about it.*"

"You're my friend, little miss know-it-all," Meg said out loud, "I failed you. I told you that I would keep my barrier up to keep you from my emotional baggage. I can't even do that right!"

Mia stepped forward, but stopped as a hand on her shoulder held her back, "Let Eve do this for her."

Meg glanced over her shoulder and saw the fae warrior that's been training with Eve. He, along with Moneek, were the ones responsible for her and Red Jayne finding this place and he had the emotions of a corpse. The witch looked back at the psychic and asked, "Why didn't you tell me?"

"*You're reacting to your trauma and not thinking right. Kind of like how I get at times. Everyone is worried about you, especially your furry companion.*"

Both Meg and Eve snorted and laughed, confounding everyone else. Mia looked at the fae warrior and he impassively shrugged his shoulders, "She's talking and Meg is listening."

"You need to go with her. This is a big deal, your first time leaving here. Just know that I understand what you're feeling and thinking. Fal'destion has been sneaking me outside, trying to aid me." Eve looked up at the witch with watery, bloodshot eyes, *"I feel like a failure to him and now, you."*

"But you're not a failure," Meg spoke. She glanced at everyone, glaring, "Do any of you think otherwise?"

A chorus of no's filled the corridor as both Axel and Victor approached. They glanced uncomfortably at each other as the larger shifter spoke, rubbing the back of his muscular neck, "So, is the mission scrubbed? What's going on?"

The vampire smirked, "A meltdown that would make Chernobyl look like a campfire."

"Piss off, fang boy!" Meg hissed which caused Victor to laugh.

"Are we going out or having a pity party tonight?" The vampire asked as he crossed his arms behind his back, grinning.

Before Mia could say a word, Meg hopped up and barked, "Yes, we are, but if you want to hang back and share your feeling with the rest of the group, I'll understand." She stormed past the scowling vampire and stuck her tongue out at him, "Undead crybaby!"

Victor turned and grabbed Meg. He tossed her over his shoulder and quipped, "If we wait for her to get to the garage, we might as well stay here. Come along, witch, and no spewing."

As the vampire sped off with the witch over his shoulder, the others dispersed after them. Eve didn't want to get up just yet as Moneek stepped back into the corridor. He looked down each end before puffing out a breath of relief, "At least that little crisis has been averted."

"She's in need of respite. This was too much for her," Fal stated as he looked down at the little psychic.

"I'm fine," Eve bit out, her lips trembling, "Neither of you don't have to be here. I don't need two mother hens. The doctor said I'm good."

The demon kneeled down by Eve as he rubbed her back, "Maybe so, but I'd like to take you somewhere for a while. Disconnect from this place."

"If I leave the facility," the little psychic looked at him, her eyes filled with dread, "*he* will find me."

"If that happens, then we can work together and end his existence. No more looking over your cute little shoulders, wondering if he's lurking in the shadows."

"Both of you love the idea of using me as bait a little too much for my liking." Eve retorted.

"Your demon is a coward. He will wait until the opportunity presents itself before he makes another play for you. This will work." Fal stated calmly.

"Besides," Moneek offered, "you're much stronger than he will ever be. We can't expect you not to be afraid. He managed to do that long ago, but now's your chance to take the fight to him. Show him that you're not a pushover."

"Where do you want to go?" Eve held her breath, anticipation eating away at her.

"Ah, ah, ah," the demon smiled mischievously, wiggling a finger at her, "That would ruin the surprise."

Eve wrapped her arms around her chest, huffing, "I don't care much for surprises."

"Hmmm, I know how to entice you to do this. But, nah. You wouldn't want it." Moneek said as he stood, watching Eve to see if she would bite. She eyed him for a moment before replying, "What are you talking about, demon?"

"Just a way to break the bond between you and your teacher. I'm sure that you don't want that."

The little psychic quickly hopped to her feet, her eyes brightened so much that the demon could actually see happiness in them for the first time. She looked between Fal and

Moneek several times, squealing with delight as she did a happy dance.

"Oh please, take me now! I can't wait for it!" Eve cried, but then her cheeks flushed as Moneek leered her way.

The demon smirked as he wiggled his eyebrows suggestively, "If you play your cards right, I will happily take you, Eve."

Eve rushed over to the demon and hugged him tightly. She spoke while inhaling his strawberry scent, "Whatever payment that you require, I will gladly give it. Just end my torment once and for all."

Moneek's lips parted as he pushed the little psychic away from him. He leaned down and pressed his forehead against hers, "You may not like the process involved so I want you to think about it before you offer me anything."

"I understand. I also know that this is something that you can't do out of the *goodness* of your heart. Demons require payment for everything."

He sighed, "It's my choice to accept payment. I don't want one. I just want you to be safe and free for once in your life."

"But," Eve stammered, her emotions were all over the place, "that's not right. From what I learned, -"

Moneek cut her off, "If the information came from *him*, then consider it false and skewed in his favor. I consider you a friend and I care about you. A lot."

Eve looked into his pleading eyes and saw that the demon was tearing up. She wasn't sure if she could trust him. Moneek hadn't done anything to bring her harm, yet. The little psychic narrowed her eyes and listened to his thoughts. She was caught off guard when she heard, "*Please, I'm not that kind of demon. I'd gladly lay down my life so she wouldn't feel an ounce of pain. I don't know if she'll ever accept me, but I will always be there for her. No matter what she accuses me of, I'll still love her.*"

"Eve? What're you thinking about," Moneek asked with concern.

She smiled and looked away, "Nothing. So, how will this bond breaking go? Will it hurt?"

"There's always a chance of pain when breaking bonds. If done wrong, death follows. I say that we kill the demon so this doesn't need to happen." Fal spoke up. He eyed the demon and asked, "How will you do it and what is required?"

"I know of a healer that can do it. I need to take her back to my people's dimension, though. Her tormentor won't be able to get in." The demon looked at Eve and added with a gulp, "I want to show her that there's good demons. It may change her mind, but if not, I'll still be by her side whether she trusts me or not."

The little psychic could feel his apprehension, he desperately wanted her to see him in a different light. She rolled her shoulders and, with determination, replied, "You might as well try and make me a believer. Will it be hot? Do I need to change into something more comfortable?"

Moneek's mouth dried as he rubbed his hand over his mouth. His thoughts were completely unguarded and she could sense his lustful images bubbling over. She was both scared and turned on at the same time.

"Can I trust you to behave or do I need a chaperone for this trip?" Eve spoke mentally to the demon as she coyly smiled.

The demon's eyes widened in surprise, he mentally stammered back, *"Oh, umm. I'm sorry for the impure thoughts. I want you so badly. Uh, what I mean, fuck I'm mucking this up! I want to show you that I'm not a bad demon. I want to show you where I live so you can judge for yourself."*

"Okay, take me then," Eve spoke out loud, and then added mentally, *"Play your cards right and I may let you try some of those images on me later."*

Eve felt bad for the demon, a thought that she never knew that she would have, ever. He squirmed under her mental flirt, which she found adorable for some reason. It was like seeing the shy kid in class getting attention from the most attractive and alluring female in the room. Eve didn't consider herself as this woman, but in Moneek's mind, she was just that and so much more.

She wanted to feel guilt for invading his private thoughts, but it was hard not to. The demon wasn't even making the effort to stop her, something that she found interesting. It was like his chance to allow the little psychic to read him like a book. Moneek was *that* comfortable with her.

Eve leaned in and tentatively hugged him and said, "Thanks. Can we go there now?"

Fal'destion nodded at the demon and asked, "You sure that her tormentor won't breach your dimension?"

"I have his magical signature. I'll give it to the gatekeepers. He can try, but," he looked directly at Eve when he felt her head move to look at him, "it will be painful and will be imprisoned if he keeps at it. Our wardings keeps dark entities like *him* out. We prefer a peaceful existence."

Fal walked over and clamped his hand on the demon's shoulder and nodded. He glanced at Eve as he said, "I will leave you to it then. You will be surprised when you get there, Eve. I know that I was when I first went there."

The fae warrior turned on his heels and walked away. Eve took a deep breath as Moneek said, "Hold on tight. I'll have to teleport us both there. Let me know when you're ready to go break the bastard's claim to you."

Eve squeezed the demon's body, inhaling his strawberry scent. Calmly she said, "Let's go and turn to a new chapter in my life. One without pain."

The demon grunted as he teleported them away from the facility.

Chapter Sixteen

Eve felt her stomach threatening to empty as they both materialized. Moneek held her, not caring if she puked on him or not. She looked around and asked, "Is this your home?"

"It's the pocket dimension that I live in. My actual home is further in there," the demon pointed at a shimmering doorway, "past the gate. Shall we?"

Eve let go of the demon and walked in tandem with him. She felt his callous hand touching the small of her back. The little psychic smiled, enjoying it. This felt like an adventure to her, a spontaneous trip to an unknown destination. Eve wasn't sure what to expect and it had her both anxious and excited.

As they came to the gate, a demon stepped in front of it. Eve watched on silently as the two demons greeted one another, speaking in demonic tongue. The gatekeeper kept glancing at the little psychic, his facial expressions switched between happy, irritation, and sympathy.

The gatekeeper finally turned his full attention to Eve and said, "Let me be the first to welcome you here, Ms. Driskell. You may come and go as you please. Don't fret, I'll ensure that no one else comes through to harm you."

Eve meekly nodded as she replied, "Thank you. I appreciate it and your hospitality."

The gatekeeper stepped aside and allowed the duo to enter. Eve heard the other demon speak to Moneek again in his demonic tongue and laughed jovially, smacking him on his back. The little psychic wondered what he said, but decided not to inquire. She was surprised at what she saw, her mouth gaped open.

Everywhere she looked was clean and tidy. The streets were made of cobblestone and there were lamp posts that lit up the areas with a white globe of energy. Small buildings lined the sidewalks with trade shops and eateries. The sky was several shades of red and purple, which the little psychic couldn't say if it was dusk or dawn. Moneek nudged

Eve forward down the street. There were demons all around, walking without a care in the world. Some alone, while others had humans walking around with them.

She saw a couple holding hands and down a nearby alley, a female demon was making out with a male human. Eve kept sneaking glances at the alley, biting her bottom lip nervously.

"Are these people slaves or concubines?" Eve asked.

"No. They're here of their own free will. You're one of the first from Earth to step foot in here." Eve gave him a questioning look, so Moneek clarified, "There's many dimensions where humans reside other than Earth. Tell me Eve, what're you reading from the people here?"

Eve opened up her senses and got greeted with elation and happiness. Hearing the thoughts of the couple in the alley told a different story, one of lust and passion. Eve gasped as she found herself smiling. Moneek grinned, enjoying this rare side of the little psychic.

A woman came out of a shop, she waved at them as she jogged towards them. Her well-endowed chest bounced with each step until she reached them, jovially exclaiming, "Moneek! I feel like I haven't seen you in ages. How have you been?"

"I've been pretty busy on Earth these days, Darla."

Darla looked at Eve as she got up close to the demon, giving him an eyeful of cleavage and asked, "Does it happen to involve this little beauty at your side?"

"It has now," the demon smiled lovingly at the little psychic, ignoring Darla's flirtatious moves, "This is Eve Driskell."

"Hi," Eve shyly spoke, her cheeks reddening under Darla's scrutinizing gaze. She walked around them both before stopping in front of Eve. She leaned in, squinting her eyes, and said with surprise, "She doesn't bear you bond. I don't recognize it. Whom does it belong to?"

The little psychic frantically looking at her body, trying to see whatever Darla was referring to, "Where is it? I don't see it."

"And you wouldn't be able to, since those here are used to seeing it. It's like a magical brand, marking you to say that you have been claimed. Darla can see it with her third eye vision."

"What do you mean by 'third eye vision'?" Eve felt confused. She squinted at Darla, "Is she wearing special contact lenses?"

Darla chuckled, "I'm not sure what those are that you're talking about. Come on, Eve, use your third eye and you will see it."

"How can I when I don't know what it is?"

Darla's mouth gaped. She looked at Moneek and then back at the little psychic, "You truly don't know, do you? My apologies. I'm so accustomed to people knowing how to use it. I didn't know that it was possible for someone your age *not* to have it open."

"Eve is learning as she goes. The one that marked her didn't teach her anything. Just used her for her inherent gifts. It's a one-sided relationship." Moneek said, looking at Eve with sympathy.

The little psychic looked away in shame, rubbing her arm, "I'm just a stupid girl."

"I wouldn't call you that, my dear," Darla said as she reached out and touched Eve's forehead, "This one's mark is a nasty piece of work. How do you plan on removing it?"

"I don't think that I can, which is why we're here. I need to see Gavril. Is he around?"

"His shop is open. He may inquire as to why you're so keen on circumventing this bond. Gavril can be obstinate when it comes to breaking bonds."

Eve panicked, "Are you saying that there's a chance that he won't do it?"

"He's a traditionalist, but I'm sure that we can persuade him to do it by having your story read when he examines the bond. It will reveal everything that the other demon has done to you." Moneek stated as he ushered Eve down the street.

"It was nice meeting you, Ms. Driskell," Darla called out. Eve looked back and smiled. The little psychic eavesdropped on the woman's thoughts without thinking about it and heard her jealous pout, "*Lucky girl. I wish that Moneek would look at me like he does her. I missed my chance with him, I guess.*"

The little psychic smiled to herself. She wasn't sure why Darla believed that Moneek wanted her. Eve debated on telling the woman that she could have him if she wanted the demon, but something tugged at her own heart. Everyone here seemed happy and content, both the demons and their human counterparts.

Is it possible that I wrongfully misjudged Moneek? Eve thought to herself. People smiled and greeted both of them, each seemed nonjudgmental and genuinely happy to the demon. She was getting everyone's thoughts, but it wasn't as overwhelming. *Either I'm getting used to my abilities or there's more going on here that I don't know about.*

Eve believed the latter. How come she got overloaded not thirty minutes ago and yet, in this place, it filtered in with ease. Even with the magical necklace that Adoy gave her didn't fully prevent other people's thoughts from breaching her mind. Moneek kept glancing at her nervously, "It's not too much further," he pointed at a sky-blue building on the corner, "That's where we're going. Hopefully Gavril can assist us in this dire matter."

Eve shrugged her little shoulders, "I wouldn't be surprised if he didn't. I'm used to bad things happening to me. It seems like that's my lot in life. One thing that I don't understand. Make it two things."

"And those are what, baby?" Moneek wearily asked.

"How come I'm not getting a sensory overload from everyone here, like I did back on Earth?"

The demon smiled benevolently at her, "The people here are accustomed to having psychics in their midst. They've learned how to effortlessly block thoughts, but they allow the positive ones to flow freely because who wouldn't want to hear that?"

As Eve nodded quietly, the demon prodded, "What's the other thing that you don't understand?"

The little psychic's cheeks flushed. She kept stealing glances at him as she asked, "Well, why do you care about me and my well-being? I'm not special. You can have anyone that you desire, like Darla, and yet, you hang around with me. I'm sure that she could offer you more than I possibly can."

"Darla and I are friends, nothing more to it. Why would you believe that I would want her?"

"She's jealous that you have eyes for me and not her. I heard her thoughts. Darla fancies you, you know. I mean, didn't you notice how she was shoving her cleavage in your face? Like I can compete with those boulders."

Moneek stopped Eve as they got to Gavril's shop. He gently grabbed her arms, leaned down and looked directly into her eyes, "I admit that she's a bit smitten with me, but I've never felt anything for her, except friendship. You, on the other hand, are different, which makes you special."

"I'm just a mental case. Darla is the better choice. I'll just end up hurting you. I always do." Eve stated as she looked at the sidewalk, tears streamed down her face.

"Why would I want someone better," the demon lifted her head up by the crook of his fingers, "when I have the best right in front of me, Eve?"

Chapter Seventeen

"But, Moneek I -" she tried to reply but got interrupted by the shop door swinging open. The demon bellowed happily as he looked at Moneek, "Dear me. Do my eyes deceive me or is that Moneek standing at my doorstep? I haven't seen you in ages. Where have you been, boy?"

"On Earth, taking care of those that need help during the Reset," Moneek replied as he turned and embraced the other demon. He motioned to the little psychic and added, "Gavril, I want you to meet Eve Driskell."

Gavril's jubilant demeanor shifted to a serious mood when he saw Eve's brand. He narrowed his eyes as he pointed, "Who's mark is on her? I don't recognize it and I know that it isn't yours, Moneek."

"May we come in and speak in private on this matter? It's why we're here."

Gavril grumbled, unsure if he wanted to know more, but Eve blurted out as tears streamed down her cheeks, "Please, Gavril. You have to help me!" She got down on her knees, pleading, "I can't take this bond any more. I don't want to suffer at his hands. If not, just kill me and be done with it so I can know peace."

Gavril shifted uncomfortably as others on the streets and sidewalks were watching, waiting to see what would happen. He glared at Moneek, "A little notice would've been nice to get from you, boy!"

Moneek put his hands up, trying to placate the demon, "I know, but she's not been well enough to leave. The owner of the mark-"

"Shut it and come inside!" Gavril snapped, but then he pleaded with the little psychic, "Please get up, girl. Everyone's gawking and I'm not enjoying the unwanted attention."

Eve stood up with her head hung low. She meekly stepped inside the shop as the demon owner held the door open for her. Eve stopped at the threshold and sadly muttered, "I'm sorry. I didn't mean to be a bother. Stupid girl."

As Moneek followed, Gavril grabbed his arm forcefully and asked, "What's wrong with the little one?"

"Read the mark and see for yourself," Moneek whispered, "She's been through a lot and has a bad opinion of us demons. One that I'm hoping, with your assistance, to change."

"You're looking to poach her, aren't you?" Gavril spat out.

"Read the brand and tell me that you wouldn't do the same thing," Moneek hissed. He yanked his arm free from Gavril's grip as they both went inside the shop. Eve had never seen a shop like this in her entire life. There were gemstones and different kinds of crystals on display on various shelves and on the walls. Exotic fabrics that shimmered ethereally felt like silk under her touch.

Several free-standing glass cabinets lined each wall, containing what the little psychic believed were amulets and various totems. She could psychically feel the power emanating from each artifact. The flooring was comprised of pure red and gold marble. Eve leaned down and could see her own reflection on the surface.

The shop felt alive, teeming with energy. Gavril pulled out several chairs and sat them in the middle of the store. He motioned for both Eve and Moneek to sit, saying, "Have a seat. I need to gather my kit for this."

Eve tentatively sat down, watching the shop owner run up a flight of stairs that she hadn't noticed earlier. She felt a hand on her thigh, Moneek gently squeezed it and said, "Don't worry. Gavril knows what he's doing."

"Maybe so, but he has yet to say that he will help me."

Gavril stomped down the stairs, holding a small box. It had sigils and runes etched into the wood. The edges of the box were lined with what looked like strings made of pure gold. A big gemstone was nestled in the center of each side of the box, each pulsated and glowed.

He sat it down on the floor as he shifted his chair to face Eve, their knees almost touching. Gavril glared at Moneek, growling as he said, "Hands to yourself. Eve has another's mark upon her."

The demon recoiled his hand, as if he was burned, "I'm only comforting her. She's scared that you will refuse."

"As she should be. Brands and bonds are our most sacred form of connection. I don't much like the idea of reading another person's bond, let alone their brand, because of the intimacy shared in it. As far as I'm concerned, you're both looking to forsake this brand for your own selfish sexual desires." Gavril vehemently retorted. His glowing eyes bore into Eve's eyes as he growled, "How many times have the two of you fucked? I'm sure that the owner of this brand would like to be made privy to this."

Eve tore her away, rubbing her arm in shame as she weakly spoke, "Never. I'm not worth the trouble it causes others."

"So, this is your first time? Cheating on the owner of your brand? I can clearly see that you've had it for eight years, why destroy this bond? Are you bored? In need of sex from another demon because you got a bad case of the seven-year itch?"

Eve mumbled her reply, which infuriated the shop owner. He snarled at her, "Speak up, girl! Show me those infidel eyes of yours. I want you to look at me when you're being accused of a crime that's condemnable by death. Give your answer or I *will* inform the authorities."

Moneek paled. He was about to grab Eve and teleport them back to the facility, but his hand froze as he heard the little psychic mentally say, *"Don't! He will listen."*

He sat back and replied with a smile that he knew that she would feel, *"I believe you, baby! I know he will once he reads the brand. If not, I have complete faith in you, no matter what happens here."*

Eve turned her head back, coming face to face with Gavril. Her eyes dimly glowed but slowly brightened as she spoke with such pervicacity that forced the shop owner to recoil, "I said *never!* Moneek and myself haven't been having sex. He saved me from the one that marked me because I'm a stupid girl for believing that he would help me with my gifts. I was wrong for ever agreeing to having your *sacred mark* from him because all I got was pain and suffering! I've been used and abused by him any chance that he got. None of my boyfriends stuck around that long because he scared them away by making me look crazy! I'm a fucked up, stupid girl that's never been touched. I'm a virgin!"

Gavril's eyes widened as he watched the little psychic. He gulped, sensing her power growing, as he spoke, his voice shaking, "Not possible... that mark...is a lover's mate mark... this can't be..."

"Read the brand and see if she's telling the truth. I'm hoping that you will see why I need to do this, for her." Moneek stated, feeling proud of the little psychic.

Gavril nodded as he reached out and touched Eve's forehead, where the brand invisibility sat. He eyed her as he calmly whispered, "You're going to feel a pressure as I look at it. Try to keep your head still during this. If I see that you're being truthful, we can move forward to the next step."

She nodded, "I'm sorry. I'm sorry for what you're about to see. Me, the stupid psychic girl."

Gavril spoke softly in his demonic tongue. Once he stopped, Eve felt the pressure on her forehead uncomfortably building. Gavril would grunt and growl as he read the brand, his body flinched as he clenched his muscles. Moneek got up and placed his hands on Eve's shoulders as he mentally said, "*Keep your eyes closed and channel the excess magic into me, baby. Imagine it flowing through your body and into mine, like a waterfall.*"

"*Like this?*" She replied as she pushed it to him. It cascaded down from the top of her head down into Moneek's hands. She shivered as her magic entered into the demon's body, their magic intermingled together. Eve felt her core reacting, wanting more from...what?

Eve felt confused, wondering what was causing her arousal. *Was it from our magic mingling or was it because of Moneek himself?* From the back of her neck, Eve noticed something poking her back. She had her suspicion of which part of his anatomy that it sprang from. The little psychic knew that he wanted her to keep her eyes closed, so Eve rocked slightly, from side to side, while keeping her head still. A small gasp escaped from Moneek's lips, which caused the little psychic to blush and stifle a giggle fit.

Gavril removed his hand from Eve's forehead and sat back in his chair. He watched them as they seemed to be having an intimate moment in front of him. He cleared his throat, causing them to open their eyes. Gavril stood up, his visage was twisted and full of anger. He snarled as he hissed out, "I'll be right back!"

The shop owner teleported away, leaving an awkward silence between the two. Moneek took his hands away Eve's and sat back down. She saw that he was supporting a decent size bulge, straining to rip through his jeans. Eve was blushing as Gavril returned.

She looked at the demon, his visage still showed signs of anger. Gavril sat down in his chair and said, "Blasphemy! He's twisted what we consider sacred for his own selfish gains. What's worse is that he's feeding off it, as we speak."

Eve gasped, "How's he doing that? Why is he doing it?"

Gavril stood up and paced, his hatred spat out, "He's manipulated the lover's mate bond. Weaving in his *version* of love in his mark, he's able to feed off all your pain and suffering. What's worse, it's giving him the sexual pleasure that comes with the mate bond. If I do this, it will be painful and this fiend *will* know that someone is tampering with the connection. He will put up a fight, one that you'll have to battle in your mind. Your choice, Eve."

"Does this mean that you'll do it? You'll help me?"

"I want to, but there's a problem. Since you've already been marked, it will be easy for another demon to attach its mark on you. I suggest that you have another brand put in its place. Someone that you trust," He looked at Moneek and said, "Are you willing to brand her with yours?"

"I am," he proudly answered as he glanced at Eve, her eyes bulged.

"Do I not get a say in this matter? It's my body after all!" Eve bit out.

"I'm afraid not, deary," Gavril answered with a sympathetic smile, "You'll be vulnerable if and when another demon spots the opening. We live in harmony with the people here. It's what the mate bond does with couples here, it causes their feelings for one another to become more intense. Now, a demon that's ten times nastier than the one who marked you, what do you think will happen?"

"I'd be some demon's one-sided relationship slave." Eve slumped her shoulders.

"That, and much worse, as it goes on. An open mark on a human also can be seen as an escapee, one who's managed to free themselves from their master. Some died while others become familiars that the demons can force to do their bidding. Some get used as a power source, to pull magic out of at any given moment, which can mean death if too much magic is taken out. So, what do you choose, Eve?"

Eve gulped, "After hearing all that, I really don't have a choice in this matter. I have to have a demon's mark on me, no matter what."

"I'll understand if you hate me for having to bear my mark. Just know that I'm doing it because I want to protect you, baby." Moneek stoically stated as he put his hand on her shoulder, "Fal's plan to kill your tormentor would've worked, but with the revelation of the mate bond being twisted, you still would be in danger. We wouldn't have seen the threat until it was too late."

Eve teared up, "I gave up my choice when I had it placed on me so long ago. I'll forever be his stupid girl." She sighed and added, "Just do it. I just hope that you aren't just like *him*."

Chapter Eighteen

"No matter what you think of me, know that I'm *not* your tormentor. When I find him, I'll tear his black heart out for you." Moneek stated as he gently squeezed her shoulder, "I care about you, a lot."

"I know, which is why I'm going through with it," Eve said and then spoke to the shop owner, "I'm ready for you, Gavril."

"I hope so, for your sake. This demon will be furious. You'll have to fight him off until I can free his mark from you. Do you understand?"

The little psychic nodded as Moneek reminded her with a smirk, "Remember your training and give him Hell for both of us."

Gavril grabbed the ornate box from the floor and rummaged through it. He pulled out a copper bowl, a crystal that looked like a dagger, and several vials of powdery substances. He muttered under his breath as he poured the contents of the vials in the copper bowl. He held the crystal blade out and commanded, "Both of you, give me your hands. I need blood from both of you for this to bind him to you, which should force his mark to usurp the existing brand."

"Should?" Eve panicked, "You mean that you don't know if it will work for certain?"

"This kind of magic can be fickle. There's always a chance that it will fail. Your tormentor will be the deciding factor in all of this." Gavril spoke as he nicked both of their hands, drawing blood. He smeared the tip and the sides of the blade in their blood and then used it to mix the powdery substances in the copper bowl.

Puffs of smoke whisper out of the bowl, the contents sizzled when it came in contact with the blood. Gavril chanted in his demonic tongue, causing previously unseen runes etched into the copper bowl to light up.

He grabbed the back of Eve's head firmly and told her, "I'm going to hold this against the brand. It's how I will destroy it, but when it's complete I need you to ingest the brew on the blade to complete the ritual. It will ensure that your tormentor can't reattach to you for a while. I'll need you to keep him distracted so that he can't fight me. Once this is all done, that's when Moneek comes in and marks you as his mate. This will completely protect you from your tormentor's attempts to reforge his mark. Got it, child?"

"Yes," Eve weakly muttered, bracing herself. Gavril pressed the tip of the crystal blade against Eve's forehead. It glowed brightly, causing the little psychic to close her eyes. Immediately, she heard the all too familiar voice of her *teacher*.

"*Ah, there's my wayward pupil! I was beginning to wonder if you survived our little chat.*" The demon mocked, "*Now I have confirmation that you couldn't have simply died. Stupid girl!*"

"*Why did you try to kill me? What did I do wrong?*" Eve mentally replied, terrified that he would appear in front of her and take her away. She also knew that he would expect her to be this way and decided that it would be the best way to keep him occupied. Tearing her down was the demon's favorite pastime.

"I wouldn't say that I tried to kill you. Your accusatory tone wounds me, Eve. I needed to teach you a lesson, that's all."

"What lesson was that? I don't understand."

"Stupid girl! Always have been and always shall be. The lesson was so simple that an idiot such as yourself could grasp it. Apparently, I was wrong. I should've known that it was too much for your feeble mind to comprehend." Eve couldn't help crying as he went on, *"No matter what you do, no matter where you go, or where you choose to hide, I will find you. So weak and pathetic. I barely exerted myself with that little demonstration. I can show you just how much worse it will get if you don't come back to me. Wait, what exactly are you doing, Eve? Where are you so I can come and collect you?"*

Eve mentally cackled as she heard Gavril say that he almost had the brand removed. She defiantly challenged her demon as she mustered up the courage to stand up to him, *"Bold words coming from one that's barely been around for weeks. I wonder if it wasn't much of a strain or if the backlash hit you so hard that you needed to recover. I can clearly see the answer in your mind. And you have the nerve to call me weak*

242

and pathetic. Look in a mirror and keep saying those words of hate back at yourself."

"Why you ungrateful little whelp! After everything I did for you, this is how you repay my generosity? It's time for your long overdue punishment!"

Eve's head felt like it was going to explode as a massive barrage of magic traveled into her through the bond. She screamed in pain as it felt like her brain was being dipped in a lava bath. The little psychic used her psychic abilities to create a wall to slow down the attack. She smiled through gritted teeth as her tormentor growled in frustration.

The demon's rant that followed was abruptly silenced when Gavril cried out, "It's off! Open your gullet and ingest the mixture, *now*!"

Eve obeyed. She felt the lukewarm crystal slide into her mouth and she greedily swirled her tongue over it, constantly swallowing whatever came off. The little psychic grimaced and made a face like she was going to be sick, but she kept on licking and swallowing.

Moneek watched her, feeling hypnotized by the way her tongue moved, wishing that it was his rock hard member in her mouth.

Eve opened her eyes and the seductive look she cast his way caused his knees to buckle. He ran a hand over his salivating mouth as Gavril pulled the crystal blade out of her mouth and ordered, "Do you wish to add your brand to her now or later. Choose now!"

Eve nibbled on her bottom lip, wondering what he was going to say. Moneek leaned down and pressed his forehead against hers and said, "I do, but it's her decision. Her body, her choice. What's your wish, baby?"

"You couldn't ask for a better demon to be mated to than Moneek," Gavril confidently spoke, trying to encourage the union, "I can vouch that he's leagues above that piece of filth you *had* attached to you, deary."

Eve eyed the demon before her and couldn't resist inhaling his strawberry scent. She smiled and said, "Mark me now, Moneek. Just, don't make me regret it."

She felt a slight tingling where their foreheads touched and also over her heart. The little psychic wanted to ask about it, but chose to be quiet and let Moneek finish uninterrupted. The tingling grew stronger and tickled, causing both the demon and the little psychic to giggle. A tendril of magic flowed from her head down to her heart, connecting both spots.

Eve smiled radiantly as Moneek pulled back. Gavril spoke as the two of them were gazing into each other's eyes, "It was a success! The brand is in place and the mating bond is strong between both of you, which tells me that you both have feelings for one another already."

Moneek raised his eyebrows in surprise, which caused Eve to blush and look away, still grinning. Gavril slapped Moneek on his back and said with mirth, a twinkle of mischief in his eyes, "If you want that bond to become permanent, don't forget to consummate this sacred union properly. If you two know what I mean."

"What?" Eve spat out. She looked between the two demons, waiting for them to laugh hysterically, but it didn't occur. Moneek reached out and took her by the hand as he escorted Eve out of the shop, saying over his shoulder, "Thanks for your assistance. We're both grateful for fixing this little problem."

"Yeah, yeah," Gavril spoke as he stood at the doorway, "just let me know when you kill the bastard. That's how you can truly thank me. It was a pleasure meeting you, Ms. Driskell."

As the door closed, Eve pulled her hand out of the demon's grasp and backed away several paces. She narrowed her eyes at him and asked, "Was this the surprise that you had in mind? Forcing yet another bond on me so that you can have a chance to get in my pants?"

"No, Eve. This was meant to keep you safe. I won't lie when I say that I do want you, but only if you'll have me. We'll feel each other's emotions because of this new bond, which might feel confusing. If you don't want to have anything to do with me, then so be it. I would never force you to do anything that you don't want to do. I can leave you here to be safe and go back to Earth and hunt your tormentor down."

Eve panicked, "I don't want to be left alone in this strange place! I wouldn't know what to do in order to survive here!"

"Nonsense. I know that you could easily survive and thrive in this place. Now that *he* can't easily track you, do you want your surprise?"

Eve shrugged her shoulders, rubbing her arm, "This was a good enough surprise. You don't need to do anything else for me."

"This was merely a peace offering to show you that I do care about you and your well-being. The little prick can't track where you are now, so I feel that it's safe enough to take you to your surprise."

Eve peered into the demon's mind, trying to see his thoughts, but got blocked out. Moneek wagged a finger, with a grin, "Now, now. No spoilers. I can tell from your curiosity that you're interested. I'm not letting you into my thoughts until you acquiesce, baby."

Eve stuck her tongue out at the demon, "That's not fair! You said that you'd never block me from your thoughts."

"It's about as fair as letting a gorgeous little psychic use her abilities to *see* the surprise." Moneek quipped.

She crossed her arms across her chest and huffed, "Point taken. So, what can you tell me about it?"

The demon chuckled as he wiggled his eyebrows, "Let's just say that it's something worth showing you in person. Trust me, it's a relaxing spot in nature. Something that you truly deserve."

Eve felt her heart racing as the bond between them pulsated. Moneek noticed it and her reaction as well. He smiled as he lifted Eve up and cradled her against his chest, "I believe that our bond is growing stronger with the feelings that we have for one another. Come, my darling. It's time for you to get spoiled!"

She giggled as they teleported away from the demon dimension.

Chapter Nineteen

Eve kept her eyes closed, not wanting to spoil her surprise. She sighed contently, deeply inhaling as she reveled in his strawberry scent. The little psychic nibbled on her bottom lip, feeling excitement slipping into her from the bond. Eve wondered if this was supposed to happen. *Does this mean that we can experience what the other is feeling?*

She opened her eyes as she felt him lowering her to the ground. Eve kept her face buried against his solid abdomen. Moneek smiled lovingly at the little psychic while pointing, "We're not there yet. Your surprise is just beyond that crest of that hill."

Eve reluctantly pushed herself away from him. She looked at where he pointed and said, "Why not just appear there instead of here?"

He reached down and grasped her hand in his, "I wanted to have a lovely stroll in the forest first. Besides, it's better to see it this way."

They walked quietly, holding hands as they marched through the thick foliage of the forest. Eve could hear the chirping of different birds all around them. Several deer scampered away when they came too close for their liking.

The forest was teeming with life, it was damp and tranquil. Eve felt more alive out in the middle of this forest, something that she never knew was possible. No voices were bombarding her mind, the only ones that she heard were ones of curiosity. The little psychic looked around and could see otherworldly entities watching them. Eve stepped closer to Moneek as she meekly asked, "Are they going to hurt us?"

"No, they won't. They're curious as to why we're here, a demon and a woman holding hands. They don't care much for my kind, so I'm going to leave them an offering."

"What kind of offering," Eve asked, fearing the worst.

The demon felt her fear, so he replied while pulling out a small sack from his vest, "The best kind. Food and drink."

They stopped by a large stone and Moneek called out loudly, "Denizens of this forest, we come in peace. As a way of showing our gratitude for letting us enter your home, we leave here some honey bread"

He held up the bread and took a bite. The demon told Eve, "Take a bite so that they know that this offering is safe to consume."

The little psychic did as he asked. She enjoyed the sweet and soft bread with a smile. Moneek sat the honey bread down on the large stone and then reached behind it and produced a small wooden bowl. At Eve's quizzical glance, he replied, "I've been here a few times. I leave this here so I can pour the drink for them."

The demon grinned as he reached into the sack and pulled out a small bottle of *Hot Damn*. He removed the lid and held the bottle aloft, "I offer this cinnamon flavored liquor and a way of saying thanks."

He took a sip from the bottle and then handed it to Eve. She sniffed it and definitely noticed the strong cinnamon aroma. She took a sip and it burned down her throat in a good way. It was like drinking cinnamon in liquid form, while the alcohol creeps up on you at the end. The little psychic stifled a giggle as she handed back the bottle.

Eve recalled how much Meg loved her wine and that she smelled like cinnamon. She wanted to ask the demon if they could find more so she could give a bottle to the witch. Eve enjoyed how the alcohol coursed throughout her body, warming her up, and causing her to smile. She watched as he emptied the contents of the bottle into the bowl. Moneek put the empty bottle back in the sack as murmurs assailed their ears.

The demon put an arm around Eve as a female voice spoke, "Offering accepted, demon. Enjoy your stay here."

They walked up a decent grade hill, causing her to pant from exertion. Moneek kept a firm hold on the little psychic, muttering to encourage her, "We're almost there. Keep coming, baby."

"Should I close my eyes then?" Eve asked.

"I would like that, but the footing on this hill can be treacherous. Just look at the ground and I will tell you to look up when the surprise comes into view. Do you trust me to guide you?"

"I do," Eve replied as she held her head up and closed her eyes with a smile. "I don't know why, but I do. Show me that I can, Moneek?"

He stepped around and got behind the little psychic with his hands on her petite shoulders. She tried controlling her breathing, but the excitement of the unknown made it difficult to concentrate. It didn't help that she felt it from Moneek too, along with his erect member that kept poking her every so often.

She mischievously smiled as she casually reached behind her and grabbed it, eliciting a small gasp from the demon.

"Eve," Moneek rasped, "You're making this...hard to guide you... safely..."

The little psychic snorted, "*This* was already hard. I thought that I could use it as motivation to get us up this hill faster."

He groaned as she squeezed him, "Oh, baby. Someone is in a playfully naughty mood. Keep it up and I'll tear your clothes off and take you. Right here, right now!"

"Are we there yet or do I need to tug on this," Eve giggled uncontrollably as she stroked him, "harder?"

They stopped abruptly. Eve felt the heat from his body engulfing her, promising to do bad things. She shivered as she felt his lips brushing against her ear as he whispered, "Open your eyes and find out, baby."

The demon teleported away from her as she opened her eyes. Eve gasped as he motioned to a large group of steaming pools of water. Moneek stood in front of the largest of the hot springs and said with a smirk, "I told you that it was a great place to relax. Come on, baby, and join me."

Eve bit her bottom lip nervously but then, she got playful when she saw him taking off his sleeveless jacket. The little psychic sent a small wave of energy at the demon's feet, causing him to tumble over backwards into the hot spring. Moneek stood up, looking confused, until he saw her giggling uncontrollably.

He teleported himself behind her and said, "I see my baby is in a playful mood. Your turn for a little dip in the water."

"No! Please don't! I'm sorry, but I don't want all my clothes soaking wet!"

The demon hissed as he grabbed her ass firmly, "Then you best be removing them. By the time I peel my wet clothes off, I'm dunking this sweet ass in the water."

Her eyes widened as he teleported back to where he left his jacket. He tugged off his shirt, causing Eve's core to respond. "I mean it. One way or another, you're going to be wet today."

Frantically, Eve yanked her shirt over her head and let drop to the ground. She undid the button on her jeans and tugged them down. She had difficulty taking them off because she forgot about her shoes. The little psychic glanced at Moneek, who was eyeing her lustfully as he kicked off one of his boots.

Eve sat down on the damp ground and yanked each of her shoes off. She kicked out of her pants and laid them next to her shirt. The little psychic reached around and quickly unfastened her small bra and wiggled it off her body.

Eve stood up as Moneek announced, "All done! Ready for that-" he paused as the little psychic tugged her panties down, letting them pool at her ankles, "dip?"

She reached down and picked up all of her clothes, giving the demon an eyeful. He groaned, pleased by what he was seeing. Eve meekly walked over to him and placed her clothes next to his pile. She turned and said with an outstretched hand, "Will you walk with me in the spring or would you rather dunk me?"

Moneek was at a loss for words. He rubbed his hand over his salivating mouth and then he grasped her hand, tugging her towards the hot springs pool. Eve gulped, but then she gasped as her feet slipped into the hot water. It felt like a hot tub, without the little jets.

Moneek escorted her towards the deeper end. He kept eyeing her naked form, causing the little psychic to blush and cover her chest. She let her dirty blonde hair obscure her face, hoping that the demon wouldn't notice her ogling him.

He's so magnificent. I wish that I looked half as good as he does.

He turned to fully face the little psychic when the water was up to his hips, barely obscuring his engorged member. He sat down, the hot water covering most of his chest. The demon pulled her down and situated Eve on his lap.

She leaned back against him and felt like she was melting away. Her moan of pleasure escaped her lips as the hot spring relaxed her body wherever it touched. Moneek embraced the little psychic in his muscular arms and asked, "Do you like this little surprise, baby?"

"Mmhmm," Eve replied as she nestled her head in the crook of his neck, "I've always wanted to come here. I never had the time or the opportunity. I never thought that I'd be sitting here, enjoying myself."

"Are you enjoying yourself?" The demon inquired as his hands caressed her body under the water. He massaged areas that felt tight, causing the little psychic to moan in approval.

"I am. I just never thought that a demon would bring me here or be nice to me." Eve careened her head so that she could see the demon's face, "I'm sorry that I've been so hard on you. You deserve someone that isn't a complete mental case."

"Given many choices, I'd choose you in less than a heartbeat, Eve Driskell." Moneek replied, eyeing her lips intently.

"Why? I'm scarred and broken. I was a lot worse when you rescued me. Why do you want me so badly when you can have anyone else that you desire?"

"Because none of them are you," he leaned forward and pressed his lips firmly against hers. He expected her to enjoy it and then break away, but she didn't. Eve reciprocated as she twisted her body so that she could wrap her arms around the back of his neck. The demon snaked his tongue into her mouth and she greedily accepted, twirling her own with his like two lovers dancing.

The demon reached down and grasped both of his hands firmly on her ass, rhythmically rocking her against his member. Eve gasped as it rubbed her core, but didn't enter. The little psychic pressed her hips against his and grinded, causing Moneek to moan. He broke away from her ravenous lips and asked, "You keep that up and I'm going to impale you with my cock."

"Is that so?" Eve looked into his eyes as she reached down and grabbed his member roughly. She stroked it as she coyly added, "You want to put *this* inside me? Are you certain that you do? I'm sure that there's others out there that have more experience at this that can give you a better time than me."

The demon growled, "You may not have experience with this, but I'm a patient demon that can and *will* teach you everything and so much more. If you will allow it, baby."

"Isn't this, what I'm doing to you, enough permission?"

"I'd rather you say it. As I said earlier, your body, your choice. We might be playing around now, but you can easily change your mind." Moneek stated as he groaned in pleasure as Eve stroked his member harder. "I'm hoping that you won't change your mind."

The little psychic smiled as she twisted on his lap, angling the demon's swollen member at the entrance of her core, "I think that it's high time that I have some quality sexual time for once. I suppose you'll have to do it."

Moneek moaned, feeling the tip of his shaft grazing her slick core, "But I'm just a demon. If we do this, the mating bond will become permanent. I know that you have your own reservations about me, baby."

"Shhhh," Eve put a finger against his lips, "just give me the time of my life. Let's not fret over my insecurities."

Eve slowly inched his swollen member inside of her core, wincing from the size. Moneek lifted her off of his lap, much to her dismay. The demon reached a hand in the water and gently caressed her mounds.

"What are you doing?" The little psychic asked as she squirmed.

"I'm going to make you ready. We need to loosen you up down here first and when that happens," the demon's eyes glowed, "I'll fuck you ten ways to the next apocalypse. I don't want your first time to be painful. So, lay back and enjoy."

Eve nodded and obeyed the demon. Moneek pulled her up and kissed her soft lips as he slid a finger inside her core while stimulating her clit with his thumb. Eve let out several gasps, much to the demon's delight. Moneek kissed his way down Eve's neck, slowly making his way to her breasts.

He engulfed one of the little psychic's breasts. The demon suckled on it tediously, tugging it up and down as he twisted his tongue over the nipple. Eve wrapped her arms around his back, digging her nails into his skin. Moneek treated the breast with the same attention as he slid a second finger inside her slick core.

"Oh fuck! Oh damn!" Eve cried out through short gasps. She arched her back, enjoying every moment of his attention. Moneek stood up with Eve as she wrapped her legs around his waist. He eyed her possessively, his voice hoarse, "I believe that you're ready for me. Fuck knows that I am."

"Then do it before something interrupts us," Eve grinned.

The demon lustfully growled as he used his hand to guide his member just inside Eve's core. He moved it up and down, the head grazing her outer lips. Eve whimpered so Moneek devilishly asked with a cocky smirk, "Does my baby want this? Should I go deeper, my little psychic?"

"Moneek, please," she pleaded, "stop teasing me!"

"Tell me what you want me to do?"

Eve firmly pressed her lips against his. She pulled back, glaring at the demon, "Fuck me or I'll knock you on your ass and do it myself!"

Moneek grinned, "I believe you and your wish is my command, baby."

He slowly pushed his throbbing member deeper inside Eve, trying to get her use to its girth. The little psychic felt the size and pressure from it, wondering if she could actually handle it. The demon stilled his movement as he kissed Eve, murmuring, "I'm letting your body adjust, which it will, so this won't be painful. I know that it's causing discomfort, but it will pass."

"I trust you, Moneek. I know that you won't hurt me."

"I never want to either. You've endured more pain that few can say that they've experienced in a lifetime. I'd rather give you pleasure beyond imagination. Are you ready?"

Eve puffed out a breath and nodded, feeling the pressure let up some, "I think so."

"Then hold on and get ready for the fun to begin, baby."

The demon pushed deeper into her core at a slow pace at first, then he built up speed to his thrusting. Eve gasped as she wrapped her nimble little fingers in Moneek's hair. He grabbed her by her ass and forcefully pressed her into each thrust. Eve squeezed her legs tightly around his body, digging her heels into his muscular ass.

The water from the hot spring splashed against them, adding another element to their pleasure. Eve cried out, moaning as her hips bucked hard with his own movements. The demon teleported them out of the hot spring and laid the little psychic down on the damp ground. He moved her legs and let them rest on his shoulders. Moneek leaned in as far as Eve could handle and thrusted harder and faster.

"Oh God! Oh fuck!" Eve panted as she felt like her head was swimming. Pressure kept building up in her core. She noticed that the demon's shaft was pulsating and twitching.

"Ah, Eve!" Moneek cried out, "I think I'm about to explode inside you!"

"Yes! Give it to me! I want it all!"

The bond that the two of them now shared seemed to pulsate, adding even more energy and pressure to the intercourse. Eve never experienced anything like this. She'd given herself orgasms before, but never did any of them compare to what she was feeling right now. The demon roared as his climax was unleashed deep inside the little psychic.

She bucked her hips as she felt her insides being lashed from the demon's ejaculate. Her core clenched and spasmed, trying to milk as much seed out of the demon. The little psychic arched her back as her own orgasm erupted like a dormant volcano. Moneek rolled over, pulling Eve on top of his sweaty body.

They both were panting and smiling at each other. Eve felt a bit light-headed and dizzy, like the forest was spinning. She rested on top of the demon, inhaling his strawberry scent and listening to his thundering heartbeats. Eve was caught off guard when she saw a glowing strand of energy emanating from his chest. It connected to her own chest, it felt warm and safe.

"It's the lover's mate bond that you're seeing, Eve," Moneek stated as he watched her play with the tendril of energy.

"It's beautiful," she replied in awe as different sensations came from it. "Why am I seeing it now? Earlier I couldn't see the brand on me and yet, I can now."

"I'm not fully sure," the demon honestly replied, "It's strange that you could see entities and not know how to use your third eye sight. Maybe you have been using it all this time, but my brand and our lovely bonding might be the reason that you can fully see. I could be wrong. What do you think?"

"As if I know the answers to everything."

"Sure, you do. After all, you're a psychic!" Moneek quipped.

Eve stuck her tongue out at the demon as he chuckled. He hugged her tightly as he kissed her on the forehead. "Did you have a good time today, baby?"

"I couldn't have asked for a better day. You did so much for me these past few weeks.

I don't know how to thank you properly. Moneek?"

"Yes, Eve?"

"Do you think that you can love a broken, crazy girl?"

"No," the demon replied. Eve sadly dropped her head down on his chest as he added, "I only have a heart for the one in my arms."

Confused, she looked up at him and said, "But I'm-"

"Shhhh," Moneek interrupted her by kissing her lips gently, "You're not that girl any longer. You've grown into a fine young woman. The trauma is always there, but you've risen above it. That's what I see in you and I couldn't be any prouder of you for it, Eve."

"I don't see myself like that, not how you do." Eve replied as she blushed deeply.

"That's because..." The demon stammered, "I- love you, Eve Driskell."

Eve smiled as she silently hugged him. Moneek wondered if she felt the same about him, but he wasn't going to force her to say anything about it. *On her terms, not mine,* he thought as he raised up. The demon cradled the little psychic in his lap and said, "We should get dressed and head back."

Eve nodded as she scrambled to her feet. She walked over and purposefully bent over slowly. She was rewarded by a groan from the demon, "You're making me regret leaving this place already. I may take you again if you keep offering your sweet body to me."

Eve snickered as she slipped her clothes on. She kept stealing glances at Moneek, enjoying his demonic physique. He tugged his jeans on and walked over and grabbed Eve, kissing her softly.

"Excuse the dampness of my attire. Someone thought it would be fun to toss me in the drink." Moneek quipped playfully.

The little psychic blushes as she held onto him tightly, deeply inhaling his strawberry scent as he teleported them back to the facility.

Chapter Twenty

The facility was buzzing as people were scrambling about frantically. Eve wasn't sure exactly what was happening, but she could feel the stress and tension washing over her like a tsunami.

"I wonder what's going on? Can you tell, Eve?" Moneek asked.

"Not really, but something terrible has occurred."

The little psychic gasped as Gloria streaked past them, carrying Meg's limp body. "No!" Eve blurted out as she chased after the female vampire. The demon ran along beside her and asked, "What's wrong, Eve?"

"It's Meg! I think- I think she's dead!" The little psychic bit out as tears trickled down her face. They came upon a section of the corridor that split into three directions. Eve looked between each one and couldn't decide which one that Gloria took.

"She might not be dead, Eve. If the vampire had her, she would be taking her somewhere for a reason. Let's go this way?"

"Why? What makes you think that's the right way?"

"Because this leads to the medical area for critical care and magical restraints, like the room you woke up in. Come on!"

They ran halfway down the corridor before encountering the female vampire, who was walking towards them. Eve stopped a few feet in front of Gloria and asked, "What's happening? Where's Meg?"

"You haven't heard? Where have you been, little one?"

"Working on freeing myself. Please tell me," Eve stepped closer, her eyes pleading, "What happened to Meg?"

"Don't give me that look, you know I can't resist it when you use it on me, child. Meg isn't doing well. She got taken away during her first mission by a nasty creature. It poisoned her mind to use her against us. She's in bad shape, daughter."

"Can I go see her?" Eve asked.

"The medical team is fussing over her at the moment, but I'm sure when they get her stabilized you can go in." Gloria replied as she reached out and brushed several strands of loose hair from Eve's face. The little psychic could tell that the female vampire was seeing her as someone else. "Victor drank most of her blood to get most of pakalchi's poison out. Hopefully, she will make it. I know that you care about her, Elenore."

"Which room?" Moneek asked.

"Restraint room six. If you go in, she won't be in her right state of mind. A pakalchi's influence is a terrible thing, especially on those that care about the victim."

Moneek took Eve's hand and teleported them near the room. The demon eyed her for a moment and asked, "Why did she call you Elenore? Did I miss something?"

"I believe that I'm the spitting image of her daughter. She hasn't talked about it any further. I think she gets lost in those memories."

The door to the room opened and they saw Jace. He looked back at the room and said, "We're all here for you two. Make sure that you eat and rest. No sense in punishing yourself needlessly."

"Can we go in?" Eve asked.

"Dr Arnica sedated Meg so she could rest and purge the poison. Mia's in there too. She's not taking this well." Jace said, concern flashing across his countenance. Dr Arnica stepped out and quietly closed the door behind her. She saw the little psychic and demon and said, "Go in if you want. Just know that Mia isn't in the best space."

Eve looked at Moneek and said, "I need to go in, but I must do it alone."

He was about to protest, but chose to say before teleporting away, "I trust that you can handle this. I'll see you later, baby."

Eve took a deep breath and opened the door. She saw the shifter standing near the bed weeping. Her thoughts were full of guilt and sorrow. The little psychic saw Meg and her mouth gaped. There were multiple IV lines in her arms and she was deathly pale.

Mia had her arms wrapped around her waist when she felt a little timid hand touch her shoulder. The shifter didn't need to look, knowing exactly who was with her, "This is all my fault, Eve. She wouldn't be like this if- if I just-"

"Could've, should've, would've. Do you need to attack yourself since you have no one for the wolf to lash out against?"

"What do you care about what I do to myself?" Mia snarled, causing the little psychic to flinch. Her eyes glowing as her wolf showed itself.

"I don't know what happened, but you need to know that you don't have to bear this burden alone. She's special to both of us. We both love her, in our own ways. I want your permission to help watch over her."

"Why ask me that question? It's not like I can stop you." Mia asked bitterly.

"I ask because I have to. If I didn't ask, would your inner beast feel like I'm treading on its claimed mate? Poaching on its territory?"

"I don't know. I never thought about it."

"I can hear it saying *'Back off, bitch! She's mine!'* I'm just a friend and not a threat. Can we share this with you?"

Mia's emotions were all over the place. She turned and embraced the little psychic tightly, saying with a shaky voice, "Yes! I don't want to lose her. Not after I just got her as my loving mate."

"This mate thing is all new to me. I'm now mated to Moneek, if you can believe it."

She heard the shifter sniffing her as she chuckled, "Yes, I see his brand and I can smell what you two were doing not that long ago."

Eve blushed as Mia spoke, "Don't worry. It's a good thing, especially in this apocalypse, finding a mate. We all need someone, though I will say that this is a little ironic. Don't you think?"

"Trust me," the little psychic grinned slightly, "it hasn't escaped my notice. I gave him such a hard time and yet, he still wanted me." The little psychic's eyes vacantly stared up at the ceiling, "This feels like a big cosmic joke at my expense. Does this mean that I have a mate or some form of Stockholm syndrome?"

Mia pulled back and then kissed Eve on her forehead as she playfully messed up her hair, "That's for you to decide. Now run along. Be with your demon, eat and freshen up. This is my watch for now."

Chapter Twenty-One

Eve sat outside the room next to the door. She promised Mia that she would sit here and psychically feel for any changes in Meg's condition. It was her way of appeasing the shifter's wolf. One less scent around its mate. Eve wanted to be here when the witch woke up. The woman did more for her than she should've done. Meg didn't know her and yet, the witch was always there for her.

It's high time to return the favor.

A disturbance of thoughts assailed the little psychic, mostly anger, confusion and remorse. Eve stood up and picked up the phone and called the extension. The phone rang on the other end several times before Jacob answered, *"Yes, Eve?"*

"Tell the others! She's awake! Meg's awake! Make sure to let her wolf know too!"

Muffled voices came over the phone, as well as cheering, *"Consider it done."*

Eve smiled as she put the phone back on its cradle. She walked over and opened the door. She saw Meg was crying as she approached. The witch barely registered a timid hand on her forearm, it squeezed just enough to get her attention. Meg peered through her bleary vision and saw Eve standing next to the bed.

"It's good to see you finally awake. I sensed you coming to, so I called and notified everyone." Eve said, smiling meekly.

"What?" The witch exclaimed; her eyes showed fear. She yanked at her restraints, desperately trying to escape. "Release me, Eve!"

Eve gently moved her hand down and let her fingers touch the restraints, "I can't do that. I know that these aren't comfortable, it never is pleasant for me either."

"Please, Eve. You don't understand," the witch pleaded. She tried calling her magic, but nothing happened. She anxiously eyed the petite woman and asked, "What's wrong with me? My magic is gone! What did I do to it?"

"Nothing. It's the restraints, remember? I was put in these shortly after I arrived here because they neuter magical abilities." Eve sighed heavily, "It seems to be my fate no matter where I'm taken."

The thought of the others made the witch resume her escape attempt; she didn't want to see any of them. It was bad enough that Eve was in the room with her, Meg couldn't recall if she was outside during the fight.

"Since you refuse to release me-"

"I'm not refusing," Eve cut the witch angrily. The young girl barely spoke and when she did, it came out as a whisper. Meg paused, waiting for the psychic to calm down. She was still struggling with her gift, but she was getting better.

At least my head didn't explode like on Scanners, the witch thought as Eve softly spoke.

"I don't have the key or I would've done it by now." She cocked her head, eyeing the witch curiously, "Why do you want the blanket over your head?"

Meg sighed, depression setting in, "You're the psychic, you should already know. I don't-"

The door opened quickly; the many residents of the facility poured through. The witch turned away in shame, averting her eyes from everyone. She didn't want to see their disappointed looks nor their reasonable baleful gazes, especially not from *her mate.*

Before anyone spoke, Eve requested, "Unlock her restraints. She's safe and doesn't want to hurt anyone else or herself."

Meg heard Dr Arnica's confused voice answered, "But, that's not why she's in them. If you say she's okay, then I'm all for it."

The witch felt hands groping around at both her wrists and ankles as Eve softly spoke, "Sorry, it's something that I've heard too often. Condition response, I suppose."

Meg imagined the young psychic was meekly looking away, rubbing her arm. She had seen Eve do it enough in the short time that she was here. Her imagination kept going, the witch didn't want to face the eyes of her friends.

"You sure? She might be better off like this." Axel asked.

Once her hands were free, Meg yanked the blanket up, covering her head. She heard Eve answer the giant shifter, "This part is about trust. Do you trust Meg to be a good witch or do you prefer her helpless and powerless because she's an easy target to prey on?"

"What? No, I'm not like that!" Axel growled at the little psychic, which angered Meg, as he whined, "You haven't been on the receiving end of one of her magically charged punches. She broke four of my ribs! Being a shifter means that I recover faster, but bones mending hurts."

"I'll break the rest of your baby back ribs, asshole, if you keep snapping at my friend!" Meg hissed as her magic thrummed through her body once more. Despite her anger, the witch didn't dare uncover herself. Her shame seemed to supplant it and with it, came the guilt.

"At least her cheery disposition is back to baseline," Axel stated as he took six steps back.

"Meg, why are you hiding, dear?" A female voice with a southern drawl asked, which meant it was Gloria.

No response.

Victor calmly remarked, "Come on, Meg. Uncover yourself so we can see how your vampiric transformation is coming along."

Meg sprang up. She flung the blanket off the bed, wide eyed, then she fell back on the bed, moaning in pain.

"Fuck! Is that the reason for the pain?" The witch bit out as she curled up in a fetal position. She ran her tongue over her teeth, probing them for fangs.

Gloria smacked Victor on the back of his head, "See what you did? You should be ashamed."

"I'm far too old for shame in my life. Look, it got her uncovered, didn't it?" Victor remarked with a smirk.

Meg whimpered, "What's causing the pain?"

"It's a side effect of the pakalchi's poison," Dr Arnica interjected, "As I understand it, you're going to feel like this for a few more days. You may feel exhaustion and fatigue, so you're on bed rest."

"Everyone was so worried about you, Meg," Eve said as she sat down on the cold tile floor, getting eye level with the witch. "You may not believe that, but I *know* it to be true."

"But why? I've done terrible things. I attacked this place, hurt others, and..." Meg shook as she gulped hard, "killed my friend."

"No one died while you were possessed," Axel stated, but pointed at his midsection, "but I do know for a fact that you hurt me."

"Stop whining," Mia spoke, causing the witch to flinch. "You're all healed up. Meg has had it way worse than you. You'll get no sympathy here, you big baby."

Eve watched as the shifter marched in the room and sat down on the bed. Sorrowfully, Mia blurted out, "I'm so sorry, Meg. I failed you miserably. This is all my fault. Can you find it in that big, beautiful heart of yours to forgive me, my love?"

"Forgive what? I'm the evil one here, not you. Everyone would be better off if I was dead and no longer a threat. I shredded Eric. I murdered the one that tried to help me. I'm not worth saving nor anyone's pity."

Mia looked at the others, feeling confused, and back at her mate, "You were under the pakalchi's influence. None of us hold what you did against you during that time. Damnit, I should've been quicker to act when she grabbed you!"

"She doesn't see it that way," Eve stated as she rested her chin on the mattress, "Meg sees us as the victims, not herself. More guilt and shame. Meg, you're a victim in this equation. The true culprit is the pakalchi and she's the one that attacked everyone, including yourself."

"We're all here for you, Meg. You're a part of this team. Why do you think we're in here with you?" Dan stated.

For the first time, the witch truly looked at everyone. She half-heartedly snarked with a nervous laugh, "So, no torches and rope. I guess that's a good sign that I'm not going to be burned at the stake."

Mia rubbed the witch's soothingly, "I think she's still feeling the effects of the pakalchi's influence. Its goal is to feed off its victims by forcing them to break any bonds and tear relationships apart. That's why it was so strong and why it struggled when Victor drank her blood."

Meg gasped, "You actually fed on me?"

The vampire slightly shrugged his shoulders, he half smirked and sneered, "To be fair, you did offer yourself willingly to me. I was more than happy to oblige, but your blood was tainted with the pakalchi poison and it didn't sit well."

The witch chuckled, "Aww. Witch's blood gave the big, bad vampire a tummy ache? Did you not enjoy tapping the witch's brewski?"

"Feel better and I might take another sip. It was either I drain you to the brink of death or snap that pretty little neck. *That* was an order that I reserved as a last resort."

Mia glared at Gaylish, but she was unfazed, "Tough options have to be explored. There was a chance that Meg and the pakalchi would be too powerful to stop. I make no excuses. Sometimes the needs of the many out way the needs of the few. Who in here would've considered killing the witch?"

"None, Gaylish. Though Axel is still bitter that he got his ass kicked by a girl. Again." Eve commented as she playfully winked at Meg with a sliver of a smile.

Meg nodded slowly, "Being a good leader comes with a baggage cart full of shit. I don't blame you for considering it, Gaylish. We're here together to stop what's going on outside these walls and I became the enemy. Say, where's Black Jack? Is he hiding or did you guys dump him in the tunnels to torment him?"

"He's been snatched. The same time that you were taken. Fal is trying to track him down as we speak." Mia stated as she laid down behind the witch, cuddling her.

Meg nodded, "If he's not back by the time I'm able to move, I want to help with the search."

Meg moaned softly, enjoying the feel of the shifter's warm body against hers. A dark figure appeared behind the petite psychic. The robed female had everyone's attention as she spoke, "This is to be expected. As more darkness floods into this world, you're all on the front line in this fight and also targets to be taken out. Meg was lucky. Black Jack isn't faring any better. The Reset is doing its part, but a greater evil is coming."

Meg thought for a moment, recalling her time with the pakalchi, then asked, "I vaguely remember the pakalchi said that others were coming to form an alliance here. She meant that they were coming here, to be with you guys, but I know that's a lie. Is it true that some ugly nasty fucks are coming here?"

The Protector closed her eyes, concentrating, "Know that I'm the Protector because I sacrificed my mortal self to ensure that humanity had a fighting chance against not only the machinations of your governments, but to save lives for the ultimate war that is to come. The ones that the pakalchi spoke of is a real threat and will look to create their own grand armies to fully conquer this beautiful world."

"So, we have some time before that happens?" Meg asked hesitantly. Her stomach churned as the Protector's eyes opened, her violet eyes glowed brightly. A feeling of dread washed over the witch.

"No, my child. They're arriving here, walking on the Earth as we speak."

Eve stood up and meekly left the room. It was becoming unbearable, but at least she knew better than to stay in the room and suffer. *Meg will understand.*

A familiar demonic voice chuckled as it echoed in her head, causing the little psychic to freeze, "*None will ever truly understand you, Eve. Come to me now and I might let you live. Either you do it or I will slaughter all who keep you from me, stupid girl!*"

Chapter Twenty-Two

Eve frantically paced in the corridor. She wasn't sure what to do exactly or what to expect from her tormentor, other than pain. The little psychic should've known that he would come for her eventually.

She cried out as she slid down the wall and, on the floor, "Why can't I have a moment of peace? Is this too much to ask for?"

Tears trickled down her face as she heard her tormentor speaking once more, "*I know that you can hear me, Eve. Come outside so we can have a little chat. You've been off your leash for far too long. It's high time to put you back in your place, at my side.*"

Eve shook her head, not wanting to do it. She also feared that her tormentor would follow through with his threat of retribution. She buried her face in her knees, rocking silently.

A hand on the top of her head broke her out of her wallowing. Eve looked up and saw Gloria standing in front of her, along with the others that were with Meg, minus the shifter.

"What's vexing you, Eve?" Gloria asked. The female vampire looked like she was ready to tear throats out and ask questions later.

"Is it *him*?" Moneek asked as he appeared next to the little psychic, his jaw muscles twitching.

Eve meekly nodded, "Yes. He's come to collect me. He says that he's going to kill anyone keeping me from him."

"Everyone to the conference room, now!" Gaylish barked. She looked down at Eve and said, "Come along, Eve. We're not letting him hurt you any longer."

"But," the little psychic muttered as her mouth trembled, "I don't want any of you to die because of me. I'll go and -"

"You will most certainly *not*!" Gaylish commanded, causing her to flinch. She glared at the demon and commanded, "Take her to the conference room and don't let her out of your sight!"

"Come Eve," Moneek said as he reached for the little psychic. He scooped her up in his arms and said with a malicious grin, "Let's make your tormentor's life Hell for once."

The demon teleported them into the conference room, where the others were filing in. Eve was concerned that these people wouldn't want to help her. *My teacher is my problem, I should deal with him myself.*

Gaylish made her way to the wall of monitors and asked, "Do you see any signs of Eve's demon?"

Hugo searched each screen and said, "It's hard to say. Is she here? Can Eve identify him if she saw the demon on the monitors?"

Everyone turned, all eyes were fixed on the little psychic. All Eve wanted to do in that moment was to let the floor open up and swallow her. Moneek set her down and ushered her forward. Eve kept her head down. She didn't want to hear their mental voices; their stares were a good indication that they wanted this problem dealt with.

An arm draped across her shoulders as Gloria asked calmly as she pointed, "Is that him? Is this your bully?"

Eve followed and let her eyes fall on the center screen. Her tormentor stood arrogantly before her, his arms wrapped against his chest and tapping his fingers on his biceps.

"Yes, unfortunately," Eve said flatly.

"He's not alone," Hugo commented as he tried to zoom in to see if he could discern what was with the demon. Others peered over the little gremlin at the monitor, several hisses escaped as they saw that it had at least three dozen hellhounds with it. Each one was twice the size of a German Shepherd and wider than a St Bernard.

Everyone watched as several hellhounds charged forward, making easy work of a small Ferals cluster that came near the demon. Eve cringed at the gory scene that was displayed on the monitors. The little psychic sighed, "I'll go to him. This isn't your fight. No one should have to die like that, on my behalf."

"You're right," Gloria replied, "but that doesn't mean that any of us are going to allow you to go through with it alone."

"Meg would rather you have support with this matter," Mia stated as she walked in the room with the witch by her side, clutching her abdomen.

"But-"

"No one hurts my friend and gets to brag about it." Meg cut her off with a hand up, gritting her teeth from the pain. "I'll stand by your side, whether you like or not, little miss know-it-all."

"It's all moot point." Eve stated, pointing at the monitors behind her, "The moment he sees me out there, he'll grab me and teleport me off to some place. Why must all of you insist that I'm worth the risk?"

Gaylish stepped up beside the little psychic and put her hand on her shoulder, "Like it or not, you're a part of this group. It's all of our responsibility to survive and thrive during this Reset. It's time to take the fight to him since he's decided to force our hand."

Adoy walked over to Eve and held out a small piece of metal, "If you can get close enough to him. Stab him with this. It will nullify his magical abilities, but in the process, will make him more deadly. Understand?" As Eve nodded and bent down to take the weapon, the magical teacher reached up and snatched the necklace off her neck, "You won't need this anymore now that you're mated to Moneek."

She looked over at her demon lover and he said confidently, "I'll take the excess into me, like the waterfall, remember? Our mating bond works in a reciprocating manner where we can draw strength from one another. Unlike a familiar, this is beneficial to both of us. You focus on your magic and I'll handle any excess that tries to build up in you."

Eve nodded slowly, but then she looked at Meg. She cringed seeing her up and moving while in so much pain. The little psychic guiltily asked, "Will you walk me out the door? You can refuse, but I need you to do something for me."

"What does my little psychic have in mind?" Meg mischievously smiled.

"*I tell you when we go out together,*" Eve mentally replied, feeling uncertain. Meg nodded slowly as she took Eve by her hand and escorted her out of the room.

"A distraction will be needed if she's going to be literally walking up to stab her demon. I'm pretty sure he's not going to leave without making a show." Axel stated as he cracked his knuckles.

"His mongrels won't stand a chance against us all," Victor coldly uttered, "I'm game for a little hunting trip."

Mia smiled, "He came here for a fight. Let's not disappoint the idiot."

Chapter Twenty-Three

Eve walked in silence with the witch. Meg glanced at her often, confidently smiling at her for support. Without the magic necklace on, Meg's thoughts entered her mind, which was odd because she could tell that the witch had her mental shield in place. Despite her pain every thought was a form of encouragement, which made the little psychic warmly smile.

As they stopped at the main entrance, Eve looked at Meg and stoically said, "I may die tonight. I'm afraid that I'm going to freeze and not be able to stab him. I need your help with this."

"How can I help? What's the plan you've hatched in that deadly brain of yours?" Meg asked with a grimace.

"I need you to..." The little psychic wasn't sure if the witch would like it, but she forced it out before she chickened out, "Use your magic on me."

Meg leaned down and grabbed her by the shoulders, "Are you serious? I might hurt you and I don't want to *ever* do that."

"It's okay. I know that you're worried about this. I'm terrified, which is why you need to make it appear as though you spelled me. To force me to him because I'm a stupid girl that needs to deal with her own drama. He needs to have his guard down and he will sense your magic on me, I'm sure. Make it sound like you hate me and that you're kicking me out against my will."

"*Eve, I can see you. Get out here now! I tire of your pathetic games. Come out now or I'll unleash the hounds on this place and have them drag you out. Not a pleasant way to do this, but then again, you're not that bright.*" Her tormentor growled mentally.

Eve cringed, but firmly whispered, "Do it now. Shake me for good measure." The little psychic cried as she shook her head as she added, "I'm resisting. Use your magic on me and let's get this over with."

The demon watched on, smirking as his little pet was obviously freaking out. He could sense that the woman with her was a strong witch, her power was so great that he debated on taking both of them. He knew that Eve had managed to cut his link to her off. This wouldn't do. He wanted all of her power to himself. *She's mine after all.*

He giggled as he saw the witch slap Eve across his face, causing his member to grow. He mentally commanded some of the hellhounds to be prepared. He wasn't going to leave this place empty handed.

The door opened with Eve being pushed out of the door by the witch. Meg glared at the demon as she called out with a hand on Eve, "Take this sniveling little shit out of here! She does more harm than good. Get moving, girl! Go give your demon a huge hug!"

Eve's eyes clouded over as she walked forward without a care in the world. The demon squinted at Eve and then asked, "What did you do, witch?"

"I used my magic on her so that she would come to you willingly. As you can see, she's being an obedient little girl."

"I like this," the demon responded, motioning to several hellhounds, "I like this so much that I'm going to take you with me. I'll reward you handsomely if you can keep Eve this placid."

As several hellhounds surrounded the witch, Meg smirked at the demon. She stepped forward, grimacing while hiking her thumb at the beasts, "No need for them. I'll join you freely. Besides, you might want to know what you're getting exactly from me."

"And what's that, witch?" The demon held his arms out as Eve got to him, coming in for a hug.

"My magic can make her do *anything* I demand. I told her to hug you and, so you can see, she's doing it with no more fussing."

"Hmm, interesting trick. One that can have many applications," the demon mused, sliding a clawed hand down Eve's back and groping her ass. "I demand another demonstration. I know how shy this one is. Make her strip."

"My pleasure, but I have to touch her for it to work." Meg said to the demon and then commanded mentally as she put a hand on Eve, "*I released my hold over you. Now shank his ass!*"

"You heard your lover, strip down and dance around him like a stupid girl!" Meg commanded as she touched her, but barely put any magic into Eve. The little psychic backed up and peeled off her clothes and let them fall haphazardly on the ground. She frolicked around the demon, causing him to groan as he rubbed himself.

Cries and howls assailed the air as the hellhounds were running around, on alert as something attacked them. The demon focused on the blurry entity that managed to shred several of the hellhounds at once.

Eve danced her way behind the distracted demon and shoved the magical blade all the way into the small of his back. Her tormentor howled in pain as he backhanded Eve. He towered over her, glaring at the little psychic. He roughly grabbed Eve by her throat and lifted her up in the air,

"Stupid girl! How dare you attack your teacher. I should rip your heart out and make you eat it for your treachery! I'll...say, who's mark is... You little ingrate! You will pay for breaking our bond! Let's leave these fools to be eaten."

The demon flinched several times with a confused look. Eve croaked out, "What's wrong... Can't flee?... This is...my chance...to teach you...a lesson..."

Eve snarled as she focused her psychic energy into her tormentor's head. It was stronger than his mental shieldings that he had in place, causing them to shatter. The demon let go of Eve, letting her drop hard on the ground. The demon clutched his head, howling in agony as the little psychic flooded his mind with every ounce of power that she could muster.

Meg grounded into the Earth and created a protective barrier, sealing herself inside with Eve and her tormentor. Hellhounds snapped and clawed at the barrier, trying to find a weakness. The twins flew by like blurs, killing indiscriminately. Mia and her pack roared violently into the fray of battle.

As the demon was digging his claws into his skull, he opened his eyes and saw a sight he had never seen before. Eve Driskell, hovering in air with her eyes glowing white and her dirty blonde hair floating all around. "Since you *love* my suffering so much," Eve coldly spoke, causing the demon to crawl back, "let me give it *all* to you! Take it, my *teacher*!"

The little psychic let all of the emotional trauma and negative energies associated with every form of abuse she ever received fuel her psychic powers. The demon screamed, holding out a pleading hand, "Stop! I beseech you! No more!"

Eve cackled maniacally, causing Meg to flinch, "I'm a stupid girl! Do you think that I can stop this? No, I'm not smart enough, you've said that numerous times. Let's see what happens when I do this! Stand up, asshole!"

To both Eve and the witch's surprise, the demon obeyed. His body spasmed and became ridged, the look of terror in her tormentor's eyes caused Eve to cackle even louder.

"You wanted me, well now you have me. Do you have something that you want to say now that we're out here?"

"Let me go, Eve," her tormentor growled painfully, "Let's have a... a civil chat."

Eve flew around the demon slowly, her fingers gliding along his stiff form, "A civil chat? Funny thing about power. When you held it over me, you took pride in my humiliation and suffering, such as having me strip naked tonight. Now, I'm the one in charge and your magic has been neutered. You can't escape *my wrath*!"

"That's impossible!" The demon squirmed under her blazing gaze, "You don't know how to do that!" He desperately attempted to call upon his magic, but nothing happened. A cold sweat broke out over his entire body. Moneek teleported himself beside the little psychic, his arm lovingly wrapped around her, "I think it's time to end this once and for all, baby."

"I think so too, my love," Eve rasped. She looked at Meg and coldly uttered, "Bubble his body. I don't want to be covered in his entrails."

More hellhounds fell as Axel grasped several, slamming them on the ground or swinging them like clubs at any hellhounds that came too close. Barbara slashed at jugulars in her panther form, circling the perimeter of the fighting, waiting for any that tried to flee. Victor snatched up a hellhound and viscously bit into its neck. He grimaced slightly, "Damn things taste like really bad eggs. Oh well, a meal is a meal."

Meg held out her hand and created a protective bubble around the demon. The witch, as well as Moneek, covered their ears as the little psychic screamed loudly. Her tormentor's body vibrated and convulsed. It was obvious that it was hurting him, but the bubble muted his cries of anguish. Small cracks split the demon's leathery skin; a pure white light emanated from within.

The fissures spread across his entire body like a wildfire. The intensity of the vibrating and the brightness of the fissures increased to the point that the demon's body exploded. Meg grimaced but quipped, "Looks like you popped that demonic hemorrhoid. Feel better, girl?"

"One moment," Eve focused on all the remaining hellhounds and froze them in place. One by one, the little psychic snapped their necks. Eve slowly lowered down to the ground, dropping to her hands and knees with her head down. She looked up at the witch as her glowing eyes went back to normal and asked, "Am I truly worth the risk? I could hurt all of you," the little psychic pointed at the demonic gore bubble, "or worse."

"You're the psychic, you tell me, little miss know-it-all?" Meg grinned as she stepped forward as she ungrounded from the Earth, "Hmm, maybe I should call you demon slayer or better yet, the demon *layer*."

Eve giggled and snorted, turning red in the face. The witch lowered her barrier and guided the bubble with the gory remains to a faraway spot and let it pop. She nearly crumbled to the ground, but Mia managed to grab her. Eve felt guilty seeing the witch like this, Meg gave so much and even when she was in excruciating pain.

The little psychic called out, "I'm sorry. I shouldn't have asked you to help me."

"Nonsense," Meg replied as she nestled up against her shifter, "You're my friend and I will do what I must to keep you and everyone here safe. You're all worth it. Now, if you don't mind, I'm going to pretend that I'm Little Red Riding Hood and have my wolf eat me, like the story goes."

Mia rolled her eyes and smirked, "Come along, where's your basket of goodies for grandma?"

Meg pointed to her crotch as they turned and walked back towards the facility, "I packed light. My, what a big mouth you got there."

Eve smiled warmly at them, then she heard the sound of someone slow clapping. The little psychic turned as she stood up and saw the twins, Victor clapping with a proud smile and Gloria hustling over with her clothes in hand.

"Spectacular work, Eve. If that doesn't say "I'm free at last!", then I don't know what will." Victor announced with a huge grin.

"Put your clothes back on," the female vampire admonished, "You'll catch your death of pneumonia. I can't lose you again."

Eve took her clothes and put a hand on Gloria's arm and said, "I'm not your daughter, but I'd like to hear more about her. Will you tell me?"

"I'm sorry. You look so much like her that I get lost in my own memories." The female vampire looked down at her hands as she fidgeted with her fingers. "You need to rest. Later, we can...talk."

Eve squeezed Gloria's arm slightly and nodded, "Thanks for your support."

Gloria sped off before tears threatened to escape. Victor stepped next to them and said with a smirk, "Get dressed or get a room. Somewhere more stimulating than amongst all these hellhound entrails, unless you two are into that sort of thing."

The vampire cackled as he ran off before either could reply. The little psychic held her clothes in her arms and looked at Moneek and said, "I'd like to go lay down. Will you join me?"

"I can never turn down an offer like that, especially from my skyclad baby." The demon grinned wickedly as he scooped her up in his arms. He kissed her passionately and murmured, "I can't say that I won't be able to keep my hands off of you. Prepare for a long night, Eve."

"Oh my," was all the little psychic could say as her demonic lover teleported them away.

Chapter Twenty-Four

Mazerth watched on silently from the shadows. The skirmish caught his attention as he passed through the area. The familiar howls of hellhounds had the lich curious. He wasn't aware that the demonic mongrels were already roaming the Earth.

The fight was informative, to say the least. The beings that won the conflict were strong and powerful and could pose a threat to himself and his comrades. Mazerth noticed a human had grabbed on to his arm and was chewing on it. The lich's eyes glowed icy blue as he commanded, "You're mine, crazed woman."

The Feral woman dropped down to the ground in a heap, convulsing violently. Her kind was easy enough to control, despite not actually being dead. The lich would add her to his hoard. When her body stopped abruptly, her eyes snapped open, glowing the same icy blue as the lich. She rose to her feet and stood quietly beside him.

Mazerth pulled out a crystal-clear dagger with a blue sapphire embedded in the bottom of the hill. The lich's eyes glowed as he muttered an incantation. Everywhere that he surveyed, the fallen hellhounds twitched and slowly rose up. They trotted over to the lich and he smiled a skeletal grin, "Come, my children."

As Mazerth turned to leave, he contemplated on telling the demon lords about what he witnessed, but dismissed it from his mind. He wanted to return to this place and *enlist* the denizens into his army.

"If I can have these powerful creatures with me, the others won't stand a chance," Mazerth mused, his emaciated form moved swiftly back into the shadows, maniacally cackling to himself.

Joshua Griffith is a Native American Cherokee who loves to tell stories about the paranormal and the supernatural, but adds a twist of humor to alleviate some of the inherent drama and suspense that can make the characters seem more relatable. He grew up in eastern part of Oklahoma, witnessing many strange and wondrous things that went bump in the night. Joshua Griffith currently resides in the Pacific Northwest. As part of his path as an energy healer, Joshua Griffith felt it would be good idea to incorporate some of his experiences in his novels. As they say, there's always a hint of truth even in a good work of fiction so it's up to you to decide which is truth and which is hot air. Joshua Griffith invites you to read his stories with an open mind because these tales are works of fiction, but ask yourself this: Could this really happen?

www.ingramcontent.com/pod-product-compliance
Lightning Source LLC
Chambersburg PA
CBHW070834280626
47161CB00015B/584